THE DEEPEST CUT

natalie flynn

Published by Accent Press Ltd 2016

ISBN 9781786151063

Copyright © Natalie Flynn 2016

In memory of Robert Knox
21st August 1989 – 24th May 2008

One

Polly found me on the landing at my dad's house, three months after my best friend Jake was murdered.

I was unconscious and lying in a puddle of my own sick.

I can't remember how many tablets I'd taken, or how much of my dad's whisky I'd washed them down with, as I hadn't bothered to keep count. I'd just kept going, downing them in threes and fours until I was too weak to lift my hand to my mouth.

I don't remember how I got from my bedroom to the landing and I don't remember throwing up, either.

All I can remember was wanting to be dead. My head had been spinning for months and I didn't know what else to do to stop it hurting. I just wanted to die.

Nobody would miss me. Jake's mum hadn't spoken to me since his funeral, and my dad only ever spoke to me to have a go at me and tell me to snap out of it. There was Polly, but I was sure she was getting fed up with me being the way I was.

When you decide you want to die, you stop thinking about anything else. You just think about that, and you wait and bide your time for the perfect chance. The day I took all the pills, my dad had left a note saying he'd buggered off away for a few days with his tart of a girlfriend, Jackie. I knew it was time. He was gone so there'd be no interruptions.

I screwed up the note and chucked it in the bin. I put the money he'd left for food in my back pocket. Then I put my duffel on and headed straight to town. The wind and rain battered me as I walked along the pavement with my hood up and head down. I felt a bit sick. I hadn't been into town since the night Jake was murdered. People would probably recognise me from the picture they'd printed of us in the papers. They might stop me and ask me questions. I knew they'd judge me.

They might even say it was my fault he died.

I went the long way round. I needed to avoid the park. The flowers people had left for Jake were long dead and put in the bin by some council street cleaner; who didn't even know him or care about him. Now there was just the bench. Our bench. Empty. It was another reminder. I didn't need to see it, not today. Not ever again.

In the second shop an old lady in the queue was staring at me. I looked the other way. She grabbed my arm with a tight grip and I tensed up.

'Are you OK, love?' She asked. 'You're shaking.'

I stayed perfectly still.

'You're poorly?' She asked. 'Got a fever? They'll sort you out,' she said, tapping the boxes of pills in my hand. 'Don't need anything fancy, just good old paracetamol.'

'Thank you,' I said quietly, with my head still down.

I paid for my pills, put them in my pocket and turned to walk out.

She grabbed my arm again. 'You feel better, lovey. Take plenty of fluids and keep warm.' She smiled then released her grip.

'Thanks,' I said. I walked away, out of the stuffy shop and back into the rain.

Why did she even care? I wanted to turn around and fling myself at her and fall into her arms and tell her that my best friend died, but then she'd know. She'd know who I was, and what I'd done, and she would stop caring about me straight away, just like everyone else.

On my way back the rain and wind were behind me, pushing me along the pavement like they were telling me to get back quickly and get on with it.

As soon as I was through the front door I grabbed dad's bottle of whisky from the kitchen side, and rushed around closing the curtains and locking the doors. I wanted to make sure nobody could see or get in. I didn't want to be saved.

Up in my room, I checked my phone. I had seven missed calls and a text from Polly. The text read: *Are you OK? Been trying to get hold of you for two days and I'm really worried Xx*. I ignored it, pulled the battery out and chucked it all in the bin in the corner of my room. I wouldn't need it anymore.

I popped all the tablets out of the blisters into a pile on my bed and swept the boxes onto the floor. I picked up the notepad I used to write my songs from the floor next to my guitar. In my bedside drawer, among all the old Top Trumps, the condoms I'd never use, and the photo of us on Jake's tenth birthday that I'd shoved there because I couldn't bear to look at it anymore, I found a pencil.

Then I wrote my suicide note. When I was done, I folded it neatly and put it under my pillow.

I took a deep breath. I was ready.

My hands were shaking as I opened the whisky and started taking the pills, just like that with my brain turned off. I wouldn't allow myself to think about it anymore. I wouldn't let me talk myself out of it. It had to be done.

I wasn't scared of dying, I was scared of living.

Polly told me after that she was worried, especially when my phone started going straight to voicemail, so she came round and she banged on the door and shouted my name and disturbed the neighbours.

'Have you seen Adam?' She asked Mrs Henderson next door, who appeared with a face like thunder asking what all the bashing and crashing was about.

Mrs Henderson just snorted and went back inside. She knew about that night, and what had happened to Jake, and what I'd done. She hated me, just like everyone else hated me. She wasn't going to help Polly.

Polly climbed over the side gate, which she told me wasn't the easiest thing to do in heeled boots in the pissing rain. She said that when she saw all the curtains shut a gut instinct kicked in; she knew something was wrong. She said it was the sort of feeling that makes you panic in every cell in your body and then your adrenalin takes over.

She kicked the back door in. It took her ages and she made

3

loads of noise.

It was Mrs Henderson who called the police – because of that. All we were to her was a bunch of reckless youths. She didn't know us, she judged us by what happened that night and by what she'd read about us in the papers afterwards. She didn't know us at all.

When Polly finally got the door in, she called my name, over and over again.

Downstairs was empty.

She ran up the stairs.

And there I was, lying there, unconscious.

Even her screaming didn't wake me up.

The police came quickly. Polly ran to the door, and pointed up the stairs. A female officer held her back as a male officer went to find me.

The ambulance came. Polly wasn't allowed to go with me. She had to stay and answer questions while some other officers secured my dad's back door.

I wasn't awake for any of this. I wasn't awake when the paramedics put me on a stretcher, when they put me in the back of the ambulance, while they put lines in and drew blood; speeding through town with blue flashing lights and a screeching siren to the same hospital they took Jake to that night. I wasn't awake while they rushed me into A&E and the paramedics handed over, telling the doctors: 'Male, seventeen, suspected overdose …'

I woke up later.

It was the bright lights that hit me first. Blinding strip lights on the ceiling. I thought I was dead. I actually thought I'd managed it.

Then a gentle female voice said, 'Ah, there you are Adam, welcome back,' and touched my hand.

I pulled my hand back. Her voice rang over and over in my ears.

I was still alive.

I pulled my oxygen mask off, the stickers off my chest and the line out of my arm, and blood spurted everywhere. I fought against the hands that were now holding me down against the bed. I hit out at anything and everything, shouting, screaming for them to get off me, to leave me alone.

They had to sedate me.

Four of them held me down and one put a needle in my thigh. A sharp scratch, then pain as the fluid went into my muscle and straight away made me go weak. My screams turned to cries. I cried and cried and cried.

I'd had one aim; and that was to kill myself to get away from the pain of losing Jake and from the guilt of what I'd done. I wanted out of this life and I'd tried really, really hard to make it happen, but I'd failed.

As I lay there crying, all I could think about was how long it would be before they'd let me out so I was free to try again.

Two

It was the pain in my stomach that woke me up.

I drew my legs to my chest and screamed out.

There were two people in the cubicle with me but I didn't know who they were. I wanted one of them to be Jake's mum, desperately. I needed her there. She'd make it all OK again. She always made everything OK again.

'Is he alright?' It was my dad's voice.

He was the last person I wanted to see. He was going to go mental at me for this, I knew it.

A nurse came in and put some clear fluid in the thing in my hand. It was cold and it stung. 'There, that should help,' she said, patting my arm. 'Just try to stay calm, OK?' She left the cubicle.

'Medically, he's stable,' a woman's voice said.

I opened my eyes to see who she was. She was in a suit and had a name tag dangling round her neck. I tried to see what it said but my eyes couldn't focus on the writing.

The pain shot through me again. I curled up in a ball and tried to breathe it away.

'Are you sure about that?' My dad asked. 'Don't really look like it, does it?'

'It's the effect of the overdose. His doctor assures me that he's stable. They're keeping an eye on his liver function, but it looks like he was found and brought here in time. He will make a full recovery.'

'He's lucky then,' Dad said.

I wouldn't call it lucky. Lucky for me would have been him identifying me in the mortuary instead of standing over my

7

sweaty, quivering body.

'We are concerned for his mental health, which is why we need to ask some questions so we can ascertain the best course of action for Adam, for when he's medically well enough to leave hospital.'

'Right,' Dad said.

I looked at him to try and see what he was thinking. He stood rigid with his arms folded over his chest and he didn't look at me.

'Do you want to take a seat?' She asked him.

'No, I'd prefer to stand.' He shifted his weight from one foot to the other.

'It might take a while.'

'Nah, I'm alright.'

She took some papers out, clicked her pen and started writing. They went through the usual stuff: date of birth, weight, and all that. I let them get on with it while I tried to stop the pain in my stomach. Then she asked the dreaded question.

'And where is Adam's mother? Are you–?'

'Deceased,' Dad said. One word. No emotion.

'When did–?'

'Three years ago.'

'Do you mind me asking how–?'

'Car accident.'

'And how has Adam been with–?'

'Fine.'

She raised her eyebrows at him and then turned her body to face me.

'Adam?'

I shrugged. There was no point trying to say how I felt with Dad standing there, because I wasn't allowed feelings. I was meant to be a man; take it on the chin, and get on with it.

'Adam, can you tell me what made you want to take an overdose?' Her voice was softer to me than it was to Dad.

I went to speak but couldn't. Even if Dad wasn't standing there glaring at me, and even if I could explain it all to her, there was no point. I didn't see the point in talking about it; or my mental health or anything else she wanted to talk about,

8

because as soon as they let me out of there I was going to jump in front of a train, or off a cliff, or hang myself. Something, anything, as long as it would definitely kill me.

She was wasting her time.

She gave me some sort of look that was halfway between a sympathetic smile and a look of worry, then she touched my hand gently and turned to my dad.

'Mr–'

'Call me Chris,' Dad said. He was staring at me with one of his looks. A threatening one: *Say anything to make me look like a bad dad and I'm gonna kill you.*

'Could you possibly shed a little light?'

'Yeah, sure. His best friend died three months ago.'

He didn't die, he was murdered.

'That's tragic, Adam. You've obviously not been coping well with losing your friend. Do you feel you could tell me what happened?'

'He was stabbed,' Dad cut in.

'Yes I think I read about that in the papers, actually.' She stopped herself. She shouldn't have said that, I could tell by the way she just stopped talking. It didn't stop the panic coming back though, because if she knew who I was, she'd stop being nice to me, even if she was being paid to be nice to me.

'Chris, could we step outside for a moment?' She turned to me, 'Adam, I'd like to have a chat with your dad in private, if that's OK with you?'

She could take him down the pub for a pint for all I cared at that moment. I had the panic back to go with the pain in my stomach, and I just wanted them to go away. I turned over and put my arm over my eyes.

They came back after a bit and Dad was pale in the face. The woman looked serious.

'Adam, with your dad's permission, I am going to go away and speak to my senior and ask them to come down and try to have a chat with you. We're concerned about your state of mind and your inability to communicate with us. We think it would be best if, when you're well enough to leave here, we transfer you to another hospital where we can keep you safe for a while,

9

until you're feeling less likely to harm yourself again.'

My dad was biting his nails. He wouldn't look at me. He'd given his permission, of course he had. I'd be out of his hair, and out of his way, and he wouldn't have to deal with me.

'How do you feel about that, Adam?' She asked. She gave me this intense look with her head cocked to the side a bit.

I nodded.

I wasn't threatened by what she just said. All I had to do was talk to her senior when they came down and convince them I was OK and, bam, I'd be out of there.

'I think you're making the right decision, we can help make you better.' She clicked her pen and put it inside her jacket pocket. 'I'll be back shortly,' she said.

Dad stared at me. He sighed. Then he left the cubicle without saying another word.

Three

I was flicking through a three-day-old newspaper when my doctor, a new doctor, a nurse and my dad came through the ward doors, making a beeline for my bed.

I put the paper down and sat up straight.

'Morning, Adam,' my doctor said. 'How are you feeling?'

Something wasn't right. Dr Sanderson had been coming in to see me every morning, just him, only him. Why was there suddenly another doctor, a nurse and my bloody dad there?

'The nurse is just going to do your vitals while we chat,' Dr Sanderson said. I held out my arm for my blood pressure. I knew the drill.

'This is Dr Verma, Adam,' Dr Sanderson said, gesturing to the other doctor. 'He's a clinical psychotherapist, and he's been helping me to decide what's best for you now you're well enough to go home.'

Dr Verma stepped forward and perched himself on my bed. 'How are you feeling today, Adam?'

I wasn't going to answer that. I was going to do what I'd been doing for the past eight days and keep my mouth shut. If I said nothing, they couldn't twist my words and accuse me of still being suicidal.

'Adam? Are you still not talking?' Dr Verma asked.

The beeping of the blood pressure monitor cut through the silence.

Dr Verma and Dr Sanderson nodded at each other. Dr Verma leant towards me.

'Adam,' he said. His voice was soft, like he was speaking to a little child. 'We're going to transfer you to a place called The

11

Meadows. It's a lovely place where you can go and take a rest for a while and …'

I didn't want to listen to anymore. I jumped up and pushed past them, dragging the blood pressure machine along with me. I ripped the cuff off my arm and threw it on the floor as Dad's arms went around my waist from behind. He was stronger than me. I struggled to get free of his grip.

'Come on now, Adam. This is for the best,' he whispered in my ear.

I elbowed him in the stomach as hard as I could and he let go.

'You little shit,' he said.

I shoved him in the chest and bolted out of the ward doors but he caught me. He grabbed me harder this time, and held me tight while the nurse caught up with us and stuck a needle in my leg.

They walked me back down the corridor, supporting me, as with every step I took I felt weaker and weaker. Whatever she'd just injected into me had the desired effect. I was now defenceless and I would have to do exactly what they said.

Back on the ward, all the other patients were staring.

Dr Sanderson drew the curtains around the bed. The cubicle was small as it was, without four more people in it. Dr Verma stared at me; Dr Sanderson at my notes. The nurse shoved a thermometer in my ear and my dad stood at the end of my bed, biting his nails and staring me out.

My jaw was tight and my breathing shallow.

I was done for. It was over. I couldn't fight them on this.

I let my eyes close, heavy from the injection, while they did whatever it was they had to do to get me put away.

I was getting locked up in the nut house and there was nothing I could do to stop it.

They took me there in a minibus ambulance. I was strapped to a wheelchair, and off my face on a second injection they'd given me just before we left. I was on my own. Dad had done a runner as soon as all the paperwork was signed. He was probably standing outside the bookies drinking a Strongbow and telling all his mates how pathetic I was.

When we pulled up, a nurse unstrapped me from the wheelchair and helped me out the ambulance.

'Whoa there, lovey,' she said when my legs wobbled underneath me. She held me upright and waited until I was steady again before we moved on.

The place didn't look like a mental hospital. It wasn't tall, dark, and looming. There was no big, dramatic entrance. There were no crazies running naked around the gardens. There were no bright flashes of lightning, no dramatic crashes of thunder, no crows squawking, threatening to peck your brains out. The building was modern and bathed in sunshine; but it didn't matter how peaceful and inviting it was, I still didn't want to go in.

'Come on, Adam,' the nurse said. She put her hand on my shoulder and walked me up the path towards the door.

She put a key code in, the door beeped, she held it open for me and we went inside.

'Come on, up the stairs,' she said, putting her hand in the small of my back.

At the top of a few flights of stairs was a set of doors with another key code thing on. She put the code in and it beeped just like the one downstairs and then she led me in.

'This is Peacock Ward,' she said. 'I'm going to show you straight to your room so you can get some rest.'

She took me down a dark corridor with no windows. None of the rooms had doors on except the bathroom. It was as quiet and peaceful inside as it was outside. It was confusing. Maybe I was the only suspected mental person in the world.

My room was one off the hallway with no door. The walls were a disgusting mustard colour and some of the paint was peeling off the white ceiling. There was a small white sink in the corner, a built-in wardrobe and a single bed. Above the bed was a small window with bars on the outside.

'No bag with you, then?' The nurse asked. 'Let me find you something clean to wear.' She walked away, her shoes squeaking along the floor as she went.

I was trapped. I knew they wanted to make me better but

they had no chance. The only thing that would make me better would be having Jake back, so unless they were God, or they had a time machine, it wasn't going to happen.

'Right, here we go.' The nurse and her squeaky shoes were back with a pair of grey joggers, a white T-shirt and a black sweater. 'They OK? I'm just going to pop and get your medication while you change,' she said.

I took off my old clothes. They stank. I'd been wearing them for the eight days I'd been in the other hospital. I put on the clean ones the nurse gave me; they were warm and comfortable.

'Pills,' she was back with a little white cup. It was the same as the ones McDonald's give you to fill up with ketchup, because they're too tight to give out packets anymore. It had two tablets in. She also had a plastic cup of water.

She handed me the pills.

'I'd like you to take these,' she said. She put the cup of water in my other hand.

I looked at the tablets and back up at her.

'They're just to help you relax,' she said.

I put them in my mouth and took some water to swallow them back.

'Poke out your tongue,' she said. She took my chin in her hand and pushed it up, looking in my mouth as she did. 'Good lad,' she said.

I gave her a funny look.

'Just checking. Get some rest,' she said. Her shoes squeaked as she walked out of the room without looking back.

That was it? Just get some rest. Nothing else. No doctor coming to see me to tell me what they were going to do with me. No family to settle me in and give me a hug. And definitely no friends to take the mickey out of me for being in the loony bin.

I was sitting there staring at the stupid yellow wall for ages. The loneliness was suffocating. However many millions and billions of people on this earth and I was on a cold bed, in a room with bars on the windows, and I had nobody. The nurses were there, but only because they were paid to be there. They didn't know what it felt like to be me. They didn't know what it felt like to be there that night, and see what happened to Jake, and do what I did. They didn't care that I couldn't think about it, because when I did, I couldn't breathe. They didn't care that I still didn't understand how it happened, how in a split second, a moment of madness, everything was destroyed.

That was what it was, a moment of madness. One quick jab of the knife and everything came crashing down around us and would never be fixed.

If that knife had never gone in, everything would have been OK.

Four

The next morning the place had sprung into life outside my room. I heard laughing, shouting, a TV, and there were smells of food, coffee, and bleach. I wasn't the only one here and I wasn't dreaming. I also hadn't died and this wasn't some warped version of the afterlife – aka hell. It was real.

I was too scared to leave my room. I mean, I'd seen my fair share of films set in mental hospitals before and they weren't exactly fun. I didn't want to get out of my bed to go and investigate; I was terrified of what I might find.

It turned out I didn't have much choice, though. A nurse appeared and told me I'd slept through breakfast, but she'd get me some tea and toast and I could have it in the therapy room while I waited for my therapist.

'Come on, up,' she said, snapping me out of the thoughts that were running around my head, like how the hell did it all come to this?

She walked me out of my room and into the corridor. I was surprised that there was nobody standing staring at a wall, or scratching their nails down it, or their own face.

The noise I'd heard had been coming from a section off the main corridor, by the nurses' station. It was full of mainly normal-looking teenagers playing pool, watching TV, and there was a game of Monopoly going on

A few stopped what they were doing and looked at me as I shuffled along behind the nurse. A couple smiled but I couldn't bring myself to smile back.

She led me into the therapy room, and inside it was just as cold and uninviting as my own room. There were just a few tables and a stack of blue plastic chairs.

'We do group therapy in here,' the nurse said. 'The one-on-one room is busy this morning, so this will have to do.'

When she walked away, saying she was off to get me some toast, I realised she reminded me of the nurse I met when Jake was in hospital when we were younger. She was cold and grumpy, too. Jake and I had pulled faces at her behind her back, but now there was no Jake there to help me make fun of her. It was just me.

The door opened and a man walked in. He was about thirty I reckon. I think he thought he was a bit of alright, and a bit cool, because he wasn't in a suit or doctors' scrubs like you'd expect. He had jeans on, and Converse, and his hair was quite scruffy like he was pretending not to make an effort with it, but you know he really had.

He held the door open for the nurse and she plonked a plate of toast and a cup of tea down on the table next to me without saying a word.

'Thank you, Anna,' the man said, nodding at her as she went out. Then he put down a pile of papers on the table, got himself a chair from the stack, and sat down opposite me.

'Hi Adam, I'm David.' He held out his hand. 'Pleased to meet you,' he said. His hand was hovering in the space between us.

I took a bite of my toast.

'So, Adam, do you know why you're here?' He pulled his hand back but he didn't look offended.

He had a weird accent. I think it might have been Irish, but it was sort of mixed in with English like he'd been over here a while and the two were blending together.

'Adam?' He picked up a pad from his papers and flicked through it to a clean page. 'How are you feeling?' He asked.

He was staring at me. It was making me nervous.

I shrugged.

'What do you remember since taking the overdose, Adam? Do you remember coming here?'

I nodded.

'And you are aware of where you are?'

I nodded again.

'OK, well you'll be with us for at least the next few weeks while we try and obtain a diagnosis and put together a treatment plan for you,' he said.

He waited for a response. I turned round to get my tea, still trying not to look at him.

'Adam,' he pulled his chair forwards a bit. The sound of it scraping on the floor made me jump.

I pulled away from him. I didn't want him near me.

'It's OK. I just want to ask you if there's any reason why you aren't talking? You haven't said a single word since you've been here. Is it on purpose? Just nod or shake your head for yes or no.'

I'd been aware of the fact I hadn't spoken to anyone, not just since I got there, but since I came round from the overdose. It was like I was numb and I just didn't have anything to say.

I tried to answer David, but I couldn't. It was the strangest sensation I'd ever felt, like my brain went to speak, but my throat wouldn't cooperate. I knew I wasn't doing it on purpose, now I'd tried to speak and couldn't.

'It's not on purpose?' David said.

I thought I'd try again but it didn't work. I suddenly felt trapped inside my own body. A feeling of dread was expanding like a huge ball in my gut. I tried to breathe deeply to calm myself down and I shook my head to tell David it wasn't on purpose.

'OK, that's OK; we can work around that, no problem.' He wrote something down on his pad. 'You OK? Just breathe through it slowly, in with three out with three ... in with three ...'

I followed his instructions until my breathing steadied.

'Take a sip of tea?'

I did as I was told.

'Right, next thing is that your dad has come in today to see you, and to have a bit of a chat with me, which I think is going to help me get a better idea of what's going on with you while you're unable to tell me yourself.' He smiled.

I knew they'd made him come. I knew him well enough to

know he wouldn't have been there out of choice. Either way, I didn't want to see him.

'Shall I go and get him? He's just outside.' I was hoping maybe he'd just *said* he was going to come but hadn't turned up at the last minute. That'd be more like him, to not turn up and leave us wondering where he was that time … the boozer, the bookies or up Jackie's arse.

David stood up. 'I think it will be good for you to see him,' he said. 'Plus, he's brought in some things for you, clothes and stuff.'

He opened the door and stuck his head out, then held open the door for my dad to come in.

Dad didn't look at me as he followed David into the room. David got Dad a chair from the stack and he sat down.

'How you doing, son?' He asked, but he still wouldn't look at me.

I stared at the floor.

'I'm missing you at home, you know. It's quiet without you around.'

What a pile of crap. David was watching him closely. I bit my nails and bobbed my leg up and down, trying to distract myself from him. I wanted to get up and walk out of the room, but I knew I had to behave the best I could and not cause a scene because then they'd let me out quicker.

Nobody was talking. The clock ticking on the wall was the only noise in the room.

David broke the silence. 'Didn't you bring some things in for Adam?' He asked my dad.

'Yeah, I've got you some bits,' Dad said to me. He shook a tatty supermarket carrier bag full of my stuff.

I didn't look up.

'That's nice of your dad, Adam, don't you think?' David asked.

There was no point in David asking me anything because I couldn't answer. I wanted him to end this and let me go back to my room and away from dad. I didn't even know why he was here. I bet he wanted to lay into me and tell me what an embarrassment and a failure I was. I bet any money that if

David wasn't there he'd be up in my face all angry and swearing.

'You sleeping alright then, son?' Dad asked, calmly.

I wished he'd drop the dad-of-the-year act – it was all for show. The last time he asked me if I was OK, or sleeping, or whatever, was the day after Jake's funeral and even that was reluctant and only because Polly was there.

'Excuse us please, Adam,' David said. 'I'm just going to have a word with your dad outside in private.' He got up from his chair and walked over to the door, holding it open for Dad who was so hot on his heels I could tell it was the greatest relief for him to be walking away from me.

I went over to the door to see if I could hear what they were saying. I needed to know so I could try and work out how long they were going to keep me in there.

'I'm afraid Adam seems to be having trouble communicating at the moment,' David said.

'I noticed,' my dad said. 'Do you know why?'

'I don't think it's on purpose. I think it could be trauma related–'

'Trauma?' Dad asked, genuinely confused.

'Mr–'

'Call me Chris,'

'Chris, you are aware of what happened to Adam's best friend, three months ago? I suspect he's suffering from what we'd call psychological trauma. How was he after the incident, before he tried to take his own life?'

'Angry, I suppose, I don't really know. I didn't really talk to him about it much …'

'Do you know if there were any nightmares at all? Panic attacks? Physical symptoms such as sweating, abdominal pain, shortness of breath?'

'Erm–'

'Any idea at all?'

'No, I don't really know, like I said we didn't really talk,' Dad said.

'Who has been supporting him through his grief, Chris?'

Silence.

Then a heavy sigh from my dad. 'Look, I just came to bring him some stuff, not to feel like I'm the one in therapy. He's the one with the issues, not me.'

'I don't want you to feel like this is an inquisition, Chris, not at all. I'm just trying to gain a better understanding of what Adam's been through, so we can start to help him. You see, the problem we have is we can't do a full psychological assessment on him until he starts communicating. Do you mind if I ask you a few more questions?'

Silence.

'OK, fine, the best I can do for him at the moment is offer him a safe environment here, and encourage him to start talking and join in group therapies. When he does, I can start to properly assess the situation and attempt to put a treatment plan in place.'

'Right,' Dad said.

'Is there anyone else that can be here to offer Adam some support?' David asked. 'It will be valuable having someone to visit him regularly, to give him stability and remind him that there is a world waiting for him outside when he's well enough to leave–'

'Debbie,' Dad said cutting in. 'Jake's mum, he spent all his life round there with them especially after my wife died,' he paused. 'There's Polly, too,' he said.

'Who is Polly?'

'Just some girl he's been knocking about with. She was the one who found him after his overdose.'

'OK, they're close?'

'Adam and Polly? I don't know, but like I said, she's been knocking about a lot.'

'Right, OK. Do you have contact details for Debbie and Polly, and are you happy for me to share the details of Adam's condition?'

I went and sat back on my chair. This was the worst kind of hell ever. They weren't going to let me out, I was trapped and there was nothing I could do.

David came back in.

'Not a massive fan of your dad, then?' He asked, sitting back

22

down.

I shook my head and he sort of smiled at me.

'It sounds to me like you've been to hell and back over the last few months,' he said.

I looked at the floor.

'Tell me, though, your dad has just mentioned Debbie, Jake's mum? I'd like to call her and tell her what's happened and see if she might want to come and see you. Is that OK?'

I straightened myself up and looked at him. I nodded but I wanted to tell David there wasn't a lot of point, that she made it perfectly clear to me at Jake's funeral that she didn't want to see me ever again. That she'd never forgive me for what I'd done. She used to be my second mum, but after that night she'd disowned me. I knew, no matter how much I wanted her to; she'd never come and see me.

'And what about Polly? Your dad mentioned you two have been spending a lot of time together since Jake … since it happened. Is she your girlfriend?'

I shook my head even though that was sort of a lie. I'd only been seeing her for a couple of weeks before it had happened. Afterwards, I had nothing to give her even if she did refuse to go away and had convinced herself that she was going to be my guardian angel and make it all better again.

'Is it OK if I tell her? Would you like to see her?' David asked and waited patiently.

I nodded because Dad was probably going to ring her anyway and tell her what had happened, if she didn't already know. For months, I had been caught in a cycle of wanting her to go away one minute but wanting her to stay the next and, at that moment, I wanted her there.

David clicked his pen and wrote something on his pad, then clicked it again and put it back into his pocket.

'I've had an idea,' he said. 'Do you want to hear it?'

I nodded.

He pulled out a brand new pad from under his pile of papers and held it out to me.

I took it off him.

'I have very limited information about what happened to

Jake,' he paused and leant forward a bit, but not too much that it made me uncomfortable. 'I do know that there was another friend, too. Nathan, yes?'

I moved my chair back and away from him and crossed my hands over my chest.

'What I want you to try and do, Adam, is to write down some stuff for me. Nothing about what happened that night just yet. I want you to tell me how you met Jake and Nathan, first.'

I put the pad on my lap.

'And maybe, if you feel you can, I'd like to know about what happened when your mum passed away. And if there was ever a time you fell out with Jake or Nathan that had nothing to do with Jake's death?' He paused. 'You think you can?' He asked.

If I did what he asked, and was on my best behaviour, maybe he'd realise I wasn't crazy and would let me out. As long as I didn't have to talk about what happened that night, I didn't mind.

'See how you feel, no pressure,' his eyebrows were raised waiting for a response.

I leant forward and took his pen out of his pocket and he smiled.

'I'll see you tomorrow,' he said. Then he left and the nurse came back in to take me back to my room.

It's funny, when you're made to sit down and think about your memories, suddenly there's not a lot you can remember. I mean, if I work it out, I've been on this earth for 365 days x 17 years, which is ... I don't know, I can't work it out in my head, but that's a lot of days and a lot of stuff that's happened to me, but I can't remember it all.

I wonder where all the memories go? Maybe there's a part of your brain, a bit like a filing cabinet, that they stay in. Some of them you can just open the drawer and pull out, but some of the drawers are locked and will stay locked forever.

Jake and I were friends since nursery school – I know that, but I can't remember much about back then, the memories are stored in a hard-to-reach place. I do know we were friends from the first day. Then our mums became friends and, because my mum worked, Jake's mum Debbie picked us up from school every day and gave us our tea, before my mum got there to take me home.

Jake and I never argued and we never fell out. We were closer than close. In year six when we were waiting to find out which secondary schools we'd got into; we were both so nervous and terrified we wouldn't get into the same one. The morning the email came to tell us I made my mum ring Jake's mum straight away to make sure Jake had got in, too. When I found out he had, we screamed down the phone to each other for ages.

We met Nathan on our first day at secondary school. We were walking up the path towards the main block when he accidentally stood on someone's foot.

'You just stood on my fucking foot,' an angry voice came from behind us, then Nathan went flying forwards into the people in front. The person whose voice it was had shoved him hard in the back.

'Sorry,' Nathan said quickly, not really sure who he was apologising to by the look of it. He was on his own, and he looked really scared. I felt sorry for him and I knew from the look on Jake's face that he did, too.

'You dickhead,' the voice came again. It was a proper deep voice. Nathan was spun around fast, so we all stopped.

'Sorry,' Nathan said again, face to face with the boy whose voice it was.

'You stood on my fucking foot,' the boy said.

'He's said he's sorry, leave it, man,' Jake said.

The boy looked Jake up and down, then he turned back to Nathan. 'Apologise to my foot,' he said, deadly serious.

Nathan went bright red. I wasn't surprised: people were watching as they walked past.

'I said apologise to my foot,' the boy said again. This time he was right up in Nathan's face. I was so embarrassed for him, but too scared to do anything about it.

'I said leave it, man,' Jake said again.

'Was I talking to you?' The boy said to Jake. 'Or was I talking to your little spastic of a friend?'

'Come on,' I said, trying to pull Jake away.

'Apologise. To. My. Foot.' The boy said louder, pulling Nathan back.

'Sorry,' Nathan mumbled and I cringed.

A teacher appeared. 'Keep it moving guys, come on, get a move on,' he said.

The boy walked off with his mates like nothing happened.

'That's William,' a girl said to us. She'd started walking next to Nathan. 'He was in our primary school and he's a right idiot. Just ignore him and stay away from him.' She smiled at Nathan, then ran off to catch up with her mates.

'You OK?' Jake asked him.

'Yeah man, what a dickhead.' He laughed. I knew he was only pretending to be OK.

'Ignore him,' I said. 'I'm Adam by the way, and this is Jake.'

He did a sort of wave. 'I'm Nathan, and thanks,' he said.

The bell went and we all went our separate ways.

At lunchtime, we saw Nathan sitting on his own reading a book. He was looking lost and lonely. It made me feel lucky to have Jake. I didn't think I'd be able to cope with the shame of sitting by myself all lunchtime.

'It must be pretty bad not having any mates,' I said to Jake. 'Shall we go over?'

'What do you think of him?' I asked.

'I dunno, let's go and find out.'

Nathan looked up from his book and seemed shocked when he saw us standing in front of him. He put the book away in his brand new, giant rucksack and smiled.

'Thought we'd come and say hi,' Jake said.

'You alright?' I asked.

He nodded.

'You tried the school lunches?' Jake asked. 'They're well rank. I'm getting my mum to do me a packed lunch tomorrow.'

Nathan laughed.

'We don't bite, you know,' Jake said. Nathan was coming across a bit snobby, like maybe he didn't really want to be talking to us. I reckoned he was just shy.

'I had a jacket potato; it was cold and hard,' Nathan said.

'Haven't you got any friends from your primary school here?' I asked him. I sat down next to him, took a bag of sweets from my pocket and offered him one. He rummaged in the bag, took a cola bottle, and smiled.

'I've just moved here,' he said. 'My dad had to move closer to work so I don't really know anyone.'

'You can hang out with us,' Jake said.

Nathan looked surprised and a bit hopeful.

I smiled at him. 'Yeah, we'll look after you.'

'Ad, that sounds well soft, should have just stuck with hanging out, man.' Jake laughed. 'Didn't he sound soft, Nath?'

'Yeah, totally,' he said, and his face broke into a huge smile and we all cracked up laughing.

'And who is this, then?' Debbie asked, as Nathan followed Jake and I into the kitchen after school.

'This, is Nathan.' Jake did a little bow at Nathan like he was presenting him to royalty and we all laughed.

'Nice to meet you, Nathan,' Debbie said, opening the fridge. 'Would you like orange juice or apple juice, and does your mum know you're here?'

I grabbed a juice carton off the side, pulled out a chair and was sitting with my feet on the table until Debbie came and slapped them off. 'Stop showing off, we've got company,' she whispered to me with wide eyes.

'Orange, please,' Nathan said quietly. He was standing by the kitchen door, and he was rubbing the back of his neck and looking at the floor.

'His mum knows, Mum,' Jake said. He opened the treat cupboard and gestured Nathan over. Nathan walked through the kitchen slowly and carefully.

'I'm sure Nathan can answer for himself, Jake,' Debbie said.

'Yeah,' Nathan said. 'She's at work till, like, eight every night, so this is better if it's OK with you. I get bored at home on my own.'

'What about your dad?' Debbie asked.

'Mum, stop with all the questions,' Jake said. His eyes were wide. He held out the chocolate bar box to Nathan.

'He works, too,' Nathan said. He picked out a KitKat. 'Thanks,' he said, waving his KitKat in Debbie's direction.

Debbie nodded. 'Brothers and sisters?'

'Sister, but she goes to a childminder. She's in primary school.'

'OK,' Debbie said, nodding. 'Well, you're always welcome to come here with Jake and Adam. Do you want to stay for dinner?'

Nathan looked at Jake, then me, for approval. We nodded.

'Yes please,' he said.

'Good,' she said. 'Right, get out of here you lot, you're under my feet.' She laughed and ushered us out of the kitchen so she could get on.

'Sorry about all the questions,' Jake said flopping onto his bed and opening his bag of crisps.

'That's OK. It's nice, you know, she cares.'

'Yeah, she does,' Jake said.

I sat down on the end of Jake's bed and opened my crisps and juice. Nathan stood in the doorway looking around Jake's room. Jake jumped up to his Xbox and turned it on.

'Do you play?' He asked Nathan.

'A bit,' he said.

Jake was holding one controller in each hand. He was biting his lip and his nose was curled up. 'I've only got two controllers,' he said.

'It's OK,' Nathan said sitting on Jake's bean bag chair. 'I'll just watch for a bit.'

Jake threw one of the controllers at me and it hit me right in the knee. I did a massive fake scream, then I leant over and smacked Jake in the arm. 'Dick,' I said.

Jake and Nathan laughed.

'What games have you got at home?' I asked Nathan.

He looked towards the window. 'I haven't really. I mostly play when I go to my cousin's house,' he said.

'Have you got a PlayStation?' Jake asked, signing in.

Nathan shook his head.

'What do you do at home, then?' He asked.

'Erm, I...'

'You don't have to have a PS4 or an Xbox, Jake,' I said. I could tell Nathan was really uncomfortable. I thought back to earlier when we'd seen him on the bench reading his book, and guessed he probably just liked reading. Maybe he wasn't that into games and stuff.

'Well, you can play here whenever you like,' Jake said. 'Do you like FIFA?'

'I love it,' he said.

'Watch me kick Adam's arse into next week, then you can try and take me on yourself. You know the controls, right?'

Nathan shrugged.

'You don't know them?' I asked. 'Have you ever played?'

Nathan shrugged again.

Jake and I looked at each other.

Nathan looked at the floor.

'Don't be sad, Nathey Boy,' Jake said. He leant over and gave Nathan a slap on the back of his shoulder. 'Now is as good a time as any to learn. But let me tell you this... you will never, ever, be as good as I am.'

'He thinks he's the king of FIFA,' I said, rolling my eyes.

'Have you ever beaten me?' Jake asked as the crowd started up and the game began.

29

'Shut up,' I said.

'Exactly.' Jake gave me a smug smile. 'Nathan, just watch, and learn,' Jake said as he booted his first goal straight in the back of the net.

The next day, at lunchtime, it all kicked off in the canteen. The school dinners weren't even fit for a dog to eat, so Jake and I brought lunch in with us. Nathan hadn't because his mum was too busy to make him one, and told him pretty much just to get on with it.

I had a bag with an apple, sandwich, and can of drink. Jake had his old *Power Rangers* lunchbox stuffed to the seams with food that Debbie had put in there, just in case we were all really hungry.

Jake had barely got the zip of his lunchbox undone when we heard William's voice singing the *Power Ranger's* theme tune.

Jake clenched his fists. I knew there was going to be trouble because I'd never seen Jake clench his fists before.

Nathan saw it, too. He had a panicked look on his face; probably thinking exactly what I was, that some serious trouble was about to go down.

William went right up in Jake's face, singing still. He was singing it. Right in his ear. All his mates were standing around laughing.

He turned to the girl in the seat next to Jake and told her to move. She looked up at him, confused. 'Move,' he shouted in her face and she got up, looking like she was about to cry, leaving her lunch where it was. William brushed it out of the way and sat down next to Jake, leaning his elbows on the table.

'Where's your lunch, then?' William asked Nathan.

None of us said anything. I was holding my sandwich mid-air, too afraid to take a bite.

'Mummy not do you a packed lunch?' William asked Nathan in a really piss-taking voice.

We all stayed silent. Ignore the bully. Ignore them. That's what we'd always been told. Then they'd go away. But he didn't.

He turned to Jake.

30

'So not quite moved up to being a secondary school boy yet, have we?' He asked, pulling the Power Rangers lunchbox towards him. 'What've we got here, then? Ooooh a chicken drumstick, oooooh another chicken drumstick ...'

I watched Jake's jaw go tight.

'Oooooooh, cold sausages and a Babybel,' William carried on. He was taking stuff out of Jake's lunchbox and passing it back to his mates. I watched Jake's face change into an expression I'd never seen on him before. I had a feeling he was about to explode. I had to man up.

'Look, can you just stop it, please?' I asked putting my sandwich down and trying to pull Jake's lunchbox back.

William laughed. 'Look at you trying to stick up for your mate. You look like you couldn't fight your way out of a wet paper bag.'

Jake shot up.

My breath caught in my throat.

Nathan's eyes bulged.

'Give me my lunchbox back,' he said. His voice was calm but steady.

William and his mates started cracking up. Silence had fallen on the area of the canteen we were in and everyone was watching us.

Jake tried to take his lunchbox back but William grabbed it and lobbed it in the corner, the rest of Jake's lunch going everywhere.

I didn't see it coming. I mean, I knew Jake was properly pissed off but I didn't see it coming. I don't think any of us saw it coming.

I heard it. The punch he landed on William's jaw. An almighty crack followed by everyone gasping. I'd never seen him that angry. I'd definitely never seen him punch anyone.

Then it erupted. The whole canteen was chanting 'fight, fight, fight' as William wrestled Jake down and they were scrapping right there in front of everyone. I looked at Nathan, and he looked back at me, and I knew we should try and stop it but neither of us was moving.

'That's enough,' a teacher shouted. I'd not seen her before.

31

She was short and dumpy and a bit sweaty. I think maybe she'd spilled some soup or something down her white, stripy shirt because there was a big red splodge on it.

A male teacher followed her into the canteen and grabbed William while she pulled Jake away, pushed him back, and stood in front of him. Her hand was hovering in front of his chest, telling him not to move. Not to try it.

When he took a step back, she looked at all of us. 'Get on with your lunches,' she shouted.

We did as she said because she was scary.

'You, out of here, now,' she said practically marching Jake from the canteen while the other teacher took William out.

After Nathan and I picked up his lunchbox, saving as much of his lunch as we could, we went up to find Jake sitting outside the staff room.

His face was angry still and he was holding his hand, the one he'd used to punch William with.

'You OK?' I asked him.

'Idiot,' he spat. Then he looked at us both. 'Not you, him.'

'Where is he?' Nathan asked, looking around.

'Medical room,' Jake said, and a small smile appeared on his face, and we all cracked up laughing.

'At least he won't mess with any of us now,' Nathan said.

'True. We got to stick together,' I said.

'And he'll know not to mess with my food again,' Jake said.

'Is that why you smacked him in the face?' Nathan asked. 'Because he messed with your lunch?'

'Nah man, my Mum made that for me. I took offence.'

I smiled at him.

'What?' He asked, rubbing his hand.

'Mummy's boy,' I said.

'Yeah, and what?'

'Out of here, you two.' The teacher came out of the staff room with a pissed-off look on her face. I couldn't take her seriously with that red splodge down her shirt. I looked at Jake and tried not to laugh.

Nathan gave Jake his lunchbox. 'It's all been all over the floor, man, you won't wanna eat it now,' he said.

'Can I go and get some lunch?' Jake asked Miss Soup Splodge or whatever her name was.

'No, you cannot.' She rolled her eyes and folded her arms in front of her chest.

'But I'm gonna be well hungry,' he said. His voice was broken.

'Well, you should have thought about that before you started a fight in the canteen.'

'He didn't start it,' Nathan said. 'William did.'

'That's not what I heard,' she said. She put her hands on her hips, cocked her head and raised her eyebrows at him.

'I need lunch,' he said.

'I don't care,' she said, not moving.

'Will he be back in lessons this afternoon?' Nathan asked.

'Nope, he's got his first date with isolation,' she said, looking straight at Jake. 'And I'll be calling your mum in a minute. Not the best way to start a new school, is it?'

Jake looked at the floor.

No lunch, isolation, and Debbie was gonna go bat shit crazy at him.

'Now get out of here you two before I find a punishment for you, as well.'

'We better go,' I said to Jake.

'Yes, you had,' she said, putting her hand on my back and moving me towards the stairs.

'See ya later,' Nathan said.

'Yeah, laters,' Jake said.

Nathan and I went off back to our lunch, wondering exactly how much trouble Jake was going to get into when Debbie found out what he'd done.

We didn't see him again till the end of school. Nathan was coming back too and we walked almost in silence. Jake was terrified about getting through the front door because he knew he was in so much trouble.

Debbie acted like nothing had happened at all, like it was just another normal day. When we left, though, that was a completely different story. Let's just say, Jake said the ceiling almost caved in with how loudly she shouted at him.

She made sure he'd never do anything like that again.

Debbie was standing at the school gates in her sunglasses, even though it was properly raining. I knew straight away that something was wrong. One, because she was wearing her sunglasses in the rain, and two, because now we were in year ten, she never ever picked us up.

It was almost Christmas. December 15th was the exact date: a date I'll never forget. We'd been counting down the days until we broke up because we were excited for two weeks off school, sitting about playing Xbox, watching movies in our pyjamas, and drinking hot chocolate.

'Why's your mum here?' I looked up at Jake from under my hood. I thought maybe something had happened with his dad, who had walked out on them when Jake was eight. Or maybe with their house or something. I never thought for a second that it might have had something to do with me.

'Dunno,' Jake said. 'Maybe she's come to pick us up 'cause it's raining or something.'

'Yeah, she looked well sorry for us yesterday when we got in all soaked and stuff,' Nathan said.

It didn't feel right. My stomach felt funny. I could feel that something was wrong.

'Alright, Mum?' Jake asked as we went over to her.

'Alright, Mrs C?' Nathan said. 'Sporting the celebrity look in your glasses, innit? You're well cool.'

She didn't laugh.

We got into the car in silence.

'Why'd you come and pick us up?' Jake asked, as he got in the front and put his seatbelt on.

I was in the back diagonal to Debbie. I was looking at her, searching for a clue. Nathan and Jake didn't seem that bothered, but my brain was going round and round.

Debbie's expression stayed the same. It didn't crack or give away any secrets. She was completely straight-faced.

'Let's just get home, OK?' She said, and turned the engine on.

Jake turned on the radio but she leant over and turned it off *again.*

'*Not now, Jake,*' *she said, but her voice was still soft as it always was.*

'*What's up?*' *Jake asked, and I could tell he was worried now, too.*

She said nothing; she just carried on driving.

Nathan looked across at me confused.

Back at Jake's, she turned the engine off. '*Jake, Nathan, when we get inside, I'd like you to go straight upstairs. I need to talk to Adam in private.*'

'*Am I in trouble?*' *I asked. I started to feel sick. There was something seriously wrong.*

She turned around. '*No, darling, you're not in trouble, not at all.*'

If I wasn't in trouble, what was this about? What had happened? I needed to know.

We undid our seatbelts and got into the house. Jake and Nathan went straight upstairs without arguing, or trying it on, or going into the kitchen for a drink and bag of crisps.

I was in the hallway, watching Debbie unzip her coat and put it on the banister. '*Let me take yours,*' *she said. She put it on the radiator to dry out.*

'*What's up?*' *I asked, but the words hardly came out, I was so scared.*

'*Let's go in here,*' *she said. She opened the living-room door and let me walk in first. Inside my dad was sitting on one of the sofas, looking at his shoes.*

'*Dad?*'

'*Sit down, son,*' *he said, but he didn't look up.*

I looked at Debbie. I was just praying that somebody would tell me what was going on.

'*I think it's best you sit down, darling,*' *she said.*

I perched on the edge of the other sofa. Debbie sat down next to me and took my hand, which was shaking.

I waited. All I could hear was the sound of my own heartbeat in my ears.

'*There was an accident this morning,*' *my dad said, but he still didn't look up.*

Debbie tightened her grip on my hand. My heart beat faster. It felt like there was a rush of something running through my body that made me feel fuzzy.

'It's your mum ...' *And that was all my dad managed to say, before his shoulders started bobbing up and down, and he started crying silently.*

I stood up but Debbie made me sit back down again.

'Is she OK, Debbie?' *I asked.* 'Is she OK?'

Debbie shook her head.

'Why? Where is she? What's happened?'

'She's in the hospital, sweetheart,' *she said.* 'She's very sick.'

'She's going to be OK, though, isn't she?' *I asked. She had to be. She had to be OK.*

Silence. Neither of them said a word.

'Dad?'

More silence.

'She was on the motorway,' *Debbie said.* 'It was a van. There was an accident.'

'Where was she going on the motorway?' *I asked. It didn't make any sense. She only worked down the road. It only took her twenty minutes to get in and back every day.* 'What motorway?' *I asked again.*

Debbie looked sternly at my dad. He said nothing.

'She had a meeting on the coast,' *Debbie told me, but still looking at my dad.*

'Can I go and see her?' *I asked.* 'I need to see her.'

'She's very sick, Adam,' *Dad said.*

'Of course you can go and see her,' *Debbie said and stood up.*

The living-room door opened, and Jake and Nathan came in.

'We're coming, too,' *Jake said.* 'We're coming, too,' *he said again. He was telling, not asking.*

'She's gonna be alright, man,' *Nathan said.* 'I promise.'

'Chris, are you going to come?' *Debbie asked.*

He shook his head.

'I think you should.'

'I can't Deb, I just can't handle it.'

36

I didn't care if he stayed or went or what he did. We started moving fast; moving to put our coats back on and out the door and into the car. I wanted to push a button to get there instantly. I needed to find out it was a mistake and, actually, she was alright and it was just a cut on the head or something. We'd laugh together about all the fuss and then go home for a fish-finger sandwich for our tea.

Luck was on our side, there was no traffic. We didn't get stuck at any lights or anything and we were there really quickly.

My mum was in the intensive-care place so Jake and Nathan couldn't come in with me; they had to wait outside in the corridor. The nurse made me scrub everything before they led me and Debbie in to see her.

She took us into a room. It wasn't like the movies, it was worse than that. There was a machine and it was going beep ... beep ... beep and it rung through my ears like it was as loud as one of those air-raid sirens. There were tubes and wires everywhere. Lying on the bed, completely still, was my mum. She was grey. There was a tube in her throat and she definitely didn't just have a cut on her head and we definitely weren't going home for a fish-finger sandwich for tea.

I stood a few feet away from the bed and looked at her.

There was no life in her at all.

I knew then that she was going to die.

I ran out of the room. It was too much to take in.

'Adam,' Debbie called after me, but I ignored her. I was scared, terrified. I didn't want to see my mum like that. It didn't look like her. It wasn't who she was. It scared me so much.

I ran down the corridor and burst through the double doors out of the ward and, right in front of where Jake and Nathan were sitting, I threw up all over the floor.

They both gasped and jumped up, then Debbie's arms went round my waist, and she held me while my whole body shook. Then she turned me around and held me tight against her chest, and stroked my hair, while I cried for what felt like hours.

'I'll never let you go,' she whispered into my ear.

The next day, when they turned off my mum's life-support machine, I was curled up in Jake's bed, under his Power

37

Rangers duvet.

I had no idea what grief was – I still don't in a way – I was only fourteen. I had no idea what I was feeling or why I was feeling it.

Mum's funeral was three days before Christmas and Jake refused to leave my side; from the moment we woke up, to the moment the hearse pulled up outside my house, and my legs went like jelly, and I fell to the floor – and all during the service, he held my hand so tight.

I sat through the whole thing, not listening to what was being said about my mum, but just staring at her coffin. I wasn't sure any of it was real. I wondered if her body was really in the coffin, a few metres away from me. I wondered how she could just die. How it seemed just like yesterday she was laughing at me, and ruffling my hair while pouring out my cereal before she left for work, and now ... Now she was lifeless, cold, gone, and locked inside that wooden box with a bunch of lilies on top. It was impossible.

I didn't cry at all during the funeral and I didn't know if that was OK, because everyone else was crying. Even my dad, even though I don't think he ever really loved my mum; not as much as I did, anyway.

After the service, Debbie took me, Jake and Nathan off to walk around the gardens and she told us that she believes in heaven. She said our souls are eternal and when we die, they're set free to go to a loving, magical place. She promised me that one day, when I'm really old and it's my turn, I will fly up to heaven and my mum will be waiting for me.

'Do you think she was in pain when she died?' I asked because it had been on my mind since it happened.

'No, I don't think she was,' Debbie said.

'I hope not,' Jake said.

'What about Christmas?' I asked, as that had been on my mind, too. I didn't want to be at home with just my dad. He'd be drunk and might not even get out of bed.

'You and your dad can spend it with us,' she said. I was pleased, but not totally, I didn't want my dad there spoiling the mood or anything. I wanted it to be just us.

We left my dad at the chapel where my mum's service was and went back to Jake's house. Debbie gave us all blankets to have on the sofa, made us hot chocolate, and closed the curtains – because she knew that was how we liked it – and, because they knew I need cheering up, Jake and Nathan let me choose the film.

Later, Debbie said I could stay over. I think she knew my dad would be in the pub, drunk. She gave us a fiver for chips and Jake and I went off back to mine to get some stuff. We said goodbye to Nathan on the corner as he went off home for his tea.

Jake and I were upstairs in my room rummaging around for some batteries for Jake's Xbox controller. I'd said I didn't really feel like playing, but he said it would cheer me up.

A key went in the lock downstairs and my dad walked in talking to someone. I heard a female voice and it made all the hairs on the back of my neck stand on end.

'Who's that?' Jake whispered as I stood in my bedroom doorway.

'I don't know,' I said, trying to listen.

The woman laughed really loudly and it was a horrible, deep, dirty laugh. It made me feel a bit sick.

'Has your dad got a bit of skirt?' Jake asked.

'No, of course he hasn't. He's with my mum,' I said. Then I realised we'd just had her funeral so he wasn't anymore. She'd only just died, though, so of course he didn't have a girlfriend yet.

'Let's go and listen,' Jake said. We walked quietly to the top of the stairs, but stayed out of view.

Dad was crashing around in the kitchen. I could tell he was drunk. I could always tell when he was drunk.

'Where's my bloody whisky?' He asked and she laughed.

'Maybe Adam has it,' she said. Who was she? I didn't recognise her voice.

'Nah, he's too much of a pussy to drink,' Dad said.

Jake was looking at me with really wide eyes. He went to speak but I put my finger to my lips to tell him to be quiet.

'So, are you going to tell him about me?' The woman asked.

My fingers and arms went numb and my heart raced. What did she mean?

A cupboard door slammed shut. 'I've just buried his mother, Jackie,' Dad said.

'I know, I know, but there's no reason for it not to be out in the open now, is there?'

'What?' Jake whispered.

'Shhhh,' I said. I didn't want to miss anything. I needed to know what they were talking about and what needed to be out in the open.

'Chris, come on,' she said. 'Is the same thing going to happen with Adam as it did with Jenny? Am I going to carry on being your dirty little secret? Just tell him for Christ sake, will ya?'

My mind felt like it had been put in the washing machine when it spins at the end.

'Your mum?' Jake whispered. Then he stopped to think. 'Do you think your dad was having an affair with that woman?'

'No, he wouldn't do that to my mum,' I whispered back. It didn't make sense.

Jake didn't look that sure and, to be honest, I wasn't that sure, either.

'She could be his long lost sister,' Jake whispered, and his voice was hopeful.

I didn't respond. I was waiting for one of them to say something else.

'I will tell him,' Dad said, less angry. 'Just not yet.'

'Oh Jesus Christ, Chris.' She was shouting.
'Shut up, will ya? What do you want me to do, ring him at Jake's and tell him right now, do ya?'

'Yeah, I think you fuckin' should.' She was screaming at him now. 'Better that than him come in and catch us at it one day, like she did. Don't want him throwing a paddy, running off, and getting flattened by a transit, do we?'

I barged Jake out of the way and I was down the stairs like thunder, and he was following me and when I got to the kitchen, they were both standing there staring at me like deer caught in *the headlights.*

'Adam,' Dad said. 'I thought you were gonna stay at Jake's?'

'Well, I'm clearly fucking not,' I shouted and some spit flew out of my mouth. I was shocked that I'd just sworn at him but I couldn't help it.

I looked at her and she was the complete opposite of my mum. She was trampy, her hair was a mess, and she had skin that looked like she spent too much time on sunbeds. She was ugly and just rough. Really, really rough. Just like him.

We were staring at each other, her and I, and I couldn't look away.

'Is it true?' I asked.

'Shall we just put the kettle on and have a cup of tea?' She asked it in a softly-softly voice, but actually, I could tell she was enjoying it – the fact I was there, and I knew, and she'd got her own way.

'Shut up,' I said to her.

'Don't be rude, Adam,' Dad said.

'Is it true?' I turned to look at him. My voice was shaking, my fists were properly clenched, and I felt like I was going to just go absolutely mental, any minute.

He looked at her.

'Is it true?' I asked again. My patience was going. My breathing was fast and shallow. One of them needed to answer my question.

He turned away from me to pour himself a drink.

'Did Mum catch you two shagging?' I asked. My voice was slow, steady. 'Is that why she was on the motorway?' It all made sense now.

He cleared his throat.

'Is that why she was on the motorway?'

Nobody was speaking apart from me.

'Somebody tell me the truth,' I screamed, so loudly I felt like my head was going to explode.

'Yes,' she said. 'She caught us and got into the car and drove off.'

'Dad?' I turned to him. My whole body was shaking.

He nodded.

I couldn't breathe. I was hyperventilating. I couldn't get any words or tears or screams out. It was their fault my mum died. Their fault.

I felt Jake's hand on my arm and he pulled me away, stepped in front of me, then squared up to my dad.

'You should be ashamed of yourself,' Jake said.

I was bent over, trying to breathe or cry or something.

Dad said nothing.

Jake turned to her. 'And you, too,' he said. Then he took me by the arm and we went straight out the front door. We walked quickly out and to the end of the street.

When we finally turned the corner, away from the house, I collapsed on the floor crying. Jake crouched down and rubbed my back until I calmed down.

That day, my life changed. My family changed in a heartbeat. I went from living happily with my mum and ignoring my bum of a dad, to being all but completely taken in by Debbie and Jake.

Jake wasn't just my friend; he was my brother.

Debbie wasn't just his mum; she was sort of my mum, too.

And that night – the night Jake died – I let them both down in a way that I knew they'd never ever do to me.

Five

'Dinner time. Didn't you hear the buzzer?' I looked up from my pad. There was a girl standing in my doorway. She was short and had frizzy blonde hair, tied back. Her clothes were all pink. Her glasses were pink, too.

'Dinnnnnnner, it's dinner time now; you can eat now, it's the proper dinner time, we have to go to the dining room and eat what they give us, and it's important that we do, or we won't get better.' She narrowed her eyes at me. 'And the tablets will make you feel sick if you don't eat, did they tell you that? They should have told you that.'

She spoke at a million miles an hour, like you'd expect a crazy person to, and it *was* mental.

The nurses had let me go back to my room after I'd finished with David. I'd stayed there writing the stuff he'd asked me to. I'd not seen or heard anyone all afternoon. Now, looking up at the girl in my doorway, I was thinking my fears about everyone in this place being mental and crazy were realistic. Maybe I should try to stay in my room as much as I could. Crazy breeds crazy, everyone knows that, and if I spent time with them maybe I'd end up turning crazy myself. I couldn't have that. I needed to keep my head down and get out of here.

'Are you coming, or not?' She said, with her hands on her hips. I had a strong feeling she wasn't going to move until I went with her.

'Come on,' she said, walking into my room, taking my hand and dragging me up. 'If you don't come for dinner you'll get in trouble, there are rules you know, and you have to stick to them.'

I had no idea where to go for dinner, so I followed her down the corridor. I was conscious of the fact I was still wearing the clothes I'd had on since I got there. I wanted a shower. I wondered if my dad had put shower stuff in the bag he'd brought in. I didn't even know where the bag of my stuff went. I'd forgotten to take it back to my room. Last time I saw it was in the therapy room.

'Hmmmmm, yummy, smells nice, doesn't it?' The girl asked. She was walking right next to me. 'I'm Caitlin by the way, what's your name?'

I looked at my feet, knowing I couldn't answer her, and felt a bit rude for it.

We passed the therapy room. I stopped and went to open the door to see if my bag was in there.

'What do you think you're doing?' Caitlin asked. She grabbed my hand and put herself between me and the door. 'That room is off limits.' She had the tone of an authoritarian headmistress, but the body of a skinny teenage girl. I wondered what she was in for. She was definitely a bit off the wall.

'Come on, you two.' A nurse ushered us to carry on down the corridor.

Caitlin rushed ahead, giving me a smug look as she went.

The dining room wasn't that big. There were a couple of blocks of tables with more of the blue chairs. I counted twelve patients. There were nurses in there supervising, too.

It was noisy, full of chatter, and everyone seemed to be behaving. Even though Caitlin was clearly mental, I'd still not seen anyone staring at walls or gouging out their eyeballs and I was pleased.

I felt like the new kid, standing by the door and not knowing quite what to do.

'Sit down, Adam,' one of the nurses said.

I sat down on an empty chair and in front of me there was a mouldy-green coloured beaker and plastic cutlery. In the middle of the table was a jug of water and some napkins.

Caitlin was sitting opposite me. A girl I didn't know was sitting next to her. We waited for a small white plastic plate of food to be put in front of us. It was a bit like being back in primary school.

It looked like tinned macaroni cheese with a very hard white roll on the side that was impossible to cut with our flimsy plastic cutlery. It didn't look the best, but I didn't care, I was starving. I put my head down to eat.

Laughter came from the corner of the room but I ignored it.

'Blake, what on earth–?'

'Blake, take those off now,' someone said. I could tell it was a nurse; it was an adult's voice. A chair scraped across the floor, shoes squeaking.

Caitlin kicked me in the shin.

I glared at her. I wasn't interested in what was going on. I just wanted to eat my dinner and get back to my room.

'Look,' she whispered, using her eyes to gesture behind her.

'That's enough, now.' The nurse's stern voice echoed across the room and the room fell deadly silent.

Three tables down, a large, goofy-looking boy, about my age, was wearing a pair of pants on his head.

I recognised those pants. They looked like the SpongeBob SquarePants ones Jake bought me for my birthday as a joke.

I put my fork down. The nurse was struggling to get my carrier bag off Blake's lap. He wouldn't let it go.

'Oh my God, Blake.' A voice cut through the silence. A teenage girl was walking towards Blake, looking so bored and so pissed off. She was tall, pretty, and had short pixie-like hair. She was in baggy joggers and a hoodie that had *London* on the front; like the sort you get on the stalls up on Oxford Street.

'You're such a retard,' she said in Blake's face. 'Gimme the bag.'

He wouldn't budge.

'Give it to me,' she screamed in his face. He jumped and let go.

'Josie,' a nurse addressed her.

'Don't worry, I've got this,' she said.

She whipped the pants off Blake's head and walked towards me with a big smile on her face.

'Yours, I believe?' She held out the bag.

My jaw was on the floor. She was amazing. She had more

control over Blake than the nurses did.

'You might wanna get these washed, though.' She put the pants in the bag. 'Don't know where Blake's been.' She winked at me.

I held out my hand and she hooked the bag over my fingers, and sat down next to me.

'Show's over, morons,' Josie shouted and the chatter returned.

I couldn't stop staring at her. I was totally mesmerised. I thought I was being a bit psycho, just staring, but she didn't seem to notice.

'I saw some scruffy-looking bloke bring that bag in earlier. I saw you on the list for therapy this afternoon, knew he was there, put two and two together, got four.'

I sort of smiled at her.

'Who was the bloke, your dad?'

I nodded.

'You hate him?'

I nodded again.

'I hate mine, too, and my mum. They got me put in here,' she sighed.

I looked at my plate. I still had some food left and wanted to eat it but thought it'd be rude while she was sitting talking to me.

'Yo, Adam,' she poked me in the arm, really hard. 'You mute?' She asked.

I nodded.

'Cool,' she said, smiling. 'I'm Josie,' she held out a small, skinny hand with really dry knuckles.

I shook it. She had a tight grip. It took me by surprise.

She leant in and whispered in my ear, 'This place can get crazy at times, but stick with me and you'll be all right.' Then she sat back, winked and smiled.

Six

I was outside.

Out of the ward.

I'd gone through the door with the keycode on it, down the stairs and out of the other door with the keycode on it. I was sitting on a bench that was a bit soggy from the rain.

I was free from the dense air of that place, free from its endless, dark corridors and my dingy room. Free from Caitlin being bossy and Blake putting my pants on his head.

The air outside smelt like rain and I was sucking it up. I sat with my face to the sky, smelling it, taking in as much of it as I could because in about five minutes, I'd be back inside that dungeon.

'Just light this, don't pull on it too much, light it and just hold it, they won't know you're not smoking,' Josie handed me the cigarette she'd just rolled. 'Make it look like you know what you're doing.' She winked.

Smokers were allowed outside, for supervised fag breaks every couple of hours, after meals and between therapy and activities, Josie had told me.

'Privileges,' she'd whispered as we were walking down the stairs behind a few of the other smokers and one of the nurses. 'If you don't smoke you aren't allowed out, so pretend.'

I'm glad she made me go out. The fresh air felt so good.
She handed me a lighter and I put the cigarette in my mouth and tried to light it.

'Pull on it a bit, but only a tiny bit,' she said. She was watching Damian, the nurse who was supervising us, to make sure he wasn't watching. 'Shit, just pull on it,' she said in a

47

whispered panic as he started to walk over.

'I didn't know you were a smoker, Adam.'

'Bit of a nosy parker, you are,' Josie said.

'Just doing my job, Josie.' He smiled.

'Well, you lot have had him doped up to his poor bloody eyeballs and locked up in there, so now he wants to enjoy a fag.'

'And he can't speak for himself?'

Josie looked up at him with her eyebrows raised. 'If you did your job properly, you'd know he was mute, so no, he can't speak for himself.'

Damian's face changed. 'I'm sorry, Adam. It completely slipped my mind,' he said.

I shrugged. There wasn't anything I wanted to say if I could.

He backed off and went over to the others.

'If I wasn't a raging lesbian, I'd fancy him a bit,' Josie said.

I wouldn't have guessed she was a lesbian. I'd never seen a real lesbian before. I'd only ever seen them in the porn films we'd watched after we hacked into Nathan's dad's computer.

We sat in silence for a bit, her smoking, me awkwardly holding a fag, which I was sure had gone out.

'Adam.' Josie turned her body around to face me and crossed her legs up on the bench. She took a long pull on her fag and then blew it out slowly.

'I heard about what happened to your friend,' she said.

My body froze, including my breathing and probably my pulse. Then panic took over and all my senses went into overdrive. My breathing and pulse raced and the blood must have been flying through my veins. I tried so hard to control it, keep it inside so she didn't see, but if she knew about me, about Jake and about what happened that night, any second, she'd tell me what a monster I was and how …

'It's OK,' she said. She touched my leg gently. It made me back away.

I wanted to get up and run away. I didn't want to hear what she was going to say to me, how she'd already judged me.

'I read it in the news, and then we had an assembly at school about it. They wanted us to know about it so we could stop it happening to us.' She paused. 'I guess they wanted to warn us.'

They'd done an assembly about us at her school? Oh God, she knew everything. She knew what I'd done. I tried to breathe deeply and slowly to keep the panic under control.

She'd got her tobacco packet out and was rolling another cigarette. 'I knew it was you when I saw your name go up on the board at the nurses' station, the day they brought you in.' She licked her paper and stuck it down.

She reached out her hand and touched my chin, pulling my head up to look at her. I flinched.

'Adam, look at me?' She asked.

I caught her eye. I didn't want to, but she wasn't giving me any choice.

'It wasn't your fault, you know that?'

I didn't want to talk about it. I shrunk down and turned away. Why wouldn't she stop talking about it? I'd been doing whatever I could to stop myself thinking about what happened, because it was like a really awful chain reaction. If I thought about it, even a little bit, the memories would start up. Then all the bad stuff would happen, feeling sick, not being able to breathe, getting all panicky, my heart racing, and my head spinning. Exactly what was happening now.

Josie was really staring at me.

I looked down at the cigarette in my hand which had gone out, but not burnt down. She held the lighter out at me and tried to smile.

I couldn't walk away from her. We were being supervised. I had to stay put. I had to be good, stay in control, not act insane or have any breakdowns or anything like that. If I kept calm, they'd let me out, I knew they would.

'It really, really wasn't your fault,' she said. She lit her cigarette and took a huge pull. 'I get it though, I do.' She blew out the smoke and batted it out of my face with her free hand.

I looked at the floor. Begging her, inside my head, to please just stop.

'Right, fag break over,' Damian announced. 'Let's all get back inside.'

Thank God. My breathing was so shallow, my pulse

thumping, my back sweating, and I felt sick. Sick like I was about to throw up everywhere.

I held out the unfinished cigarette. She took it off me and threw it in the bush. She flicked hers in after it and walked next to me back through the keycode door. Inside I took the stairs two at a time and was first through the ward door as soon as Damian opened it. I couldn't get up there quickly enough. I just wanted to go to my room and be alone.

Damian took my arm as I tried to walk away. 'Do you think you can handle staying out here for a bit, Adam?' He asked.

I was confused.

'Just, you've been in your room all day. I think it will do you good to stay out here for a bit, if you think you're up to it?'

'Wanna play pool?' Josie asked, grabbing two cues and smiling brightly.

Oh, God. I looked at Damian for an escape route.

'It'll be fun. Josie's a demon, though. She can beat anyone,' he said, either ignoring or not understanding the pleading look on my face. 'Go on. If you don't enjoy yourself, I'll let you have the chocolate bar I've got saved to go with my cup of tea later,' he said.

I didn't have a choice. I had to be good so they'd let me out.

I shuffled over to where Josie was setting up the pool table and picked up one of the cues. I'd only every played pool once before, in the pub with Jake and Nathan while we were waiting for my dad to turn up from the bookies with that week's food money. I was crap. I'd lost. Twice in a row.

Josie pulled her hoodie off and chucked it on the chair. My eyes were drawn straight to her arms which were covered in scars. Some were white, some were big and purple. Some were still scabs.

She chucked the chalk to me but I didn't catch it. My head still felt fuzzy from just being outside for the first time in ages.

She laughed as she bounced over and grabbed it from by my feet. She placed it in my palm and rolled her eyes at me. 'I'm gonna whoop your arse if you can't even catch the chalk,' she laughed. 'You wanna break?'

I shook my head. I watched as she leant over and broke the

balls perfectly. She potted a yellow then looked up at me smugly.

She caught me staring at her arms. Her hand went up and rubbed them protectively. 'You want to know?' She asked.

I was curious. She seemed so normal and strong and confident. Not the sort of person who would be locked up in this nut house and definitely not the sort of person I'd expect to do stuff like that to herself.

I went to take my turn.

'I've been doing it for ages. My parents hate the fact I'm a lesbian,' she said, while I took my shot and missed. I was still crap.

She took another shot. 'You're gonna lose, by the way.'

I shrugged. I didn't really care about playing. I was only there because Damian said so.

I lined up my cue, took a shot and missed.

'When I came out,' Josie carried on, 'my whole world was turned upside down. I had a girlfriend, you know, but 'cause I'm only seventeen, Mum and Dad thought it was just a phase, that I'd grow out of it. They thought grounding me would be the answer. Lock her up; keep her in there until she changes her mind. It's bullshit. They're my parents; they're supposed to love me no matter what, right?'

I didn't know if they were or not. My dad didn't love me no matter what.

She bent over and lined up her cue, 'It's not like I killed anyone ... Shit, sorry, Adam,' she stood up and looked at me. 'Sorry.'

I looked at the floor. I knew she didn't mean it, but it still made me feel like I'd been punched in the stomach. The thing is you can't stop people saying words like death, killed, and dying. People just say them, then realise after and feel bad, but there's nothing really to feel bad about. They just said a word, that's all. I let her carry on.

'I lost the plot, being locked up inside the house. I lost the plot, Adam. I went mental. I trashed the house, I threw stuff, I locked myself in the bathroom and slit both of my wrists.' She held out her arms.

'I've been in here since,' she said. She bent back down, lined up her cue and smacked a red straight into the far right pocket.

'Fancy grabbing us a hot chocolate?' She smiled. Her story was over, just like that. She told it all and didn't cry or panic or anything like that. I didn't get it. I didn't understand how she could be so calm about all those feelings.

I put my cue down. I didn't know where to get hot chocolate from. I looked around to see if there was a kettle or something.

'Over there,' she said. She was pointing near the nurses' station where there was a hot drinks vending machine. 'We're allowed three hot drinks a day from there, but we aren't allowed to take them back to our rooms unless we have a visitor with us. We have to drink them here. Go to the nurse and ask for a token,' she said.

I went over to the nurses' station slowly. My head was spinning again. I think Josie was trying to be my friend. I didn't need a friend. I was just keeping my head down, getting on with things, doing what they told me to do, trying to stay calm and act normal so they would let me out. The sooner they let me out of there, the better.

I didn't bother with the tokens in the end. I knew I should have stayed out there really, but Damian had only asked me to try. I'd tried. I went straight back to my room and got the pad and paper out from underneath my bed. The quicker I got all this down for David, the quicker they'd let me go.

When you've been friends with someone for ever, you never imagine them not being there. They're a part of you. Especially when you see them every day. Your life revolves around them and, everything you do and everywhere you go, they're right there with you.

That was us. That was me, Jake and Nathan. Where one was, the others weren't far behind. Except for one time in year eleven, before it all happened, right before our exams. For a moment, I thought it was all over.

It started on the day some year twelve boys lobbed my trainers up a tree by the bus stop outside school. If that hadn't happened, Jake wouldn't have got together with Kelly Dawson.

'I'm a go and get an ice pop,' Jake said as we got to the shops outside school. 'Want one?'

'Nah, I'm going to go to the chicken shop,' I said. I'd had double PE in my last two lessons and I was starving. I wanted a chicken drumstick and chips.

'You're gonna get fat if you keep eating that chicken shit all the time,' Nathan said. 'It's probably not even chicken, it's probably rat, or–'

'Nath, man, shut up.' Jake nudged him in the side and shook his head. 'Anyway, Ads, you know mum's cooking burgers tonight, yeah? Homemade juicy burgers with that Emmentalblahblah whatever it's called cheese, bacon, ketchup, tomatoes and ...'

'Yeah, I know, and I'm gonna eat them, but if I don't get chicken and chips now, I'm not gonna make it to dinner,' I said.

They laughed. ''K, meet you there,' Jake said.

Nathan went with him and I went to the chicken shop round the corner on my own. As soon as I got in there, I wanted to walk straight back out again because the place was full with the idiots from year twelve.

I stood at the back, so I didn't catch any of their eyes, and pretended to read the menu on the board over the counter. When the man asked me what I was having, I stepped forwards with my head down and told him.

I was embarrassed because my money was all in silver coins, mostly tens and twenties, but it was too late to back out because the man was already piling the chips into the box and fishing me out a drumstick.

I handed him the money with my fist closed, hoping the year twelve boys wouldn't see, but the chicken man tutted and pretty much threw it on the counter to count it all out. Really slowly.

One of the year twelve boys started laughing.

'Trampy Adam with his coppers for his chicken,' he said.

'And his cheap trainers,' another said, looking at my feet.

My face went hot. Jake and Nathan needed to hurry up. Jake would have been rummaging right in the bottom of the freezer for the best ice pop.

The year twelve boys were laughing loud. I was just about to run off, without my chicken, when one of them grabbed my foot and pulled my trainer off.

'What even are these?' He asked.

'No name, ooooooooh,' another said, and they all started laughing again.

I stood with my shoeless foot in the air. The chicken man finally finished counting my money and gave me my box of chicken, but I couldn't leave because they still had my trainer.

'Can I have my trainer back, please?'

They all laughed.

One of them grabbed my other leg and I hopped backwards while he took the other trainer off.

I was just in my socks. One of them had a huge hole in which meant my big toe was popping out.

Their laughs made my stomach churn. I didn't move, or speak. I braced myself for their next move.

One of them held my trainers as another tied the laces together. When he was done, they all ran out the chicken shop laughing.

I followed them outside. Jake and Nathan were walking towards me, sucking on their bloody ice pops with stupid, confused looks on their faces.

'Why haven't you got any shoes on, man?' Nathan asked.

Then they both clocked the year twelve boys with my trainers, running towards the bus stop.

'Oi, what you doing?' Jake shouted. He handed Nathan his

ice pop and ran after them. 'Stop it,' he said, but it was too late. With a clean throw, my shoes were dangling from a branch in the tree.

The people at the bus stop were staring. Some were trying not to laugh.

I stood there with no shoes on, holding my box of chicken, completely mortified.

The year twelve boys ran off in hysterics.

'Wankers,' Jake said.

I shielded the sun from my eyes as I looked up into the tree. 'How am I gonna get them down?' I asked. My no-name trainers were dangling from a high branch. I had to get them down, I needed them. There was no way my dad was going to buy me new ones.

Jake took his school bag off, hooked it over Nathan's head, and rolled up his sleeves.

'You're never gonna get up there, man,' Nathan said. 'Let's just go back to school, get the caretaker to bring a ladder or something?'

I couldn't speak. The people at the bus stop were still looking. I had never been so embarrassed in my whole life.

An older man from the bus stop went over to Jake. He looked like a builder. He had on one of those sleeveless vests which showed off his muscly arms, dirty shorts, and those big builder boots. 'I'll give you a leg up,' he said. His voice was really deep.

Jake got into position and the builder guy literally hoisted him up into the tree like he was light as a feather.

'There's not a lot of grip on my shoes,' Jake shouted down to us. 'If I fall, break my neck, and die, I don't want shitty hymns at my funeral, I want cool songs. You lot choose, yeah.'

I didn't laugh. I didn't find any of it funny. I just wanted my shoes back.

Jake perched himself on a branch and leant over, grabbed my shoes, hooked them off the tree and dropped them down on the floor by my feet.

'You alright?' The builder man asked Jake, looking up at him concerned. I was, too. We all knew it was easier to get up a tree than down from it and I really didn't want Jake to break his neck.

He slowly and carefully got down from the tree while I untied the knot in my laces and put my trainers back on.

Jake did the final bit with a jump, brushed himself off, and thanked the man.

'Yeah, thanks,' I said.

He gave me a sort of sympathetic smile.

'Back to the shop,' Jake said, taking his bag off Nathan.

'Why?' I asked.

'My ice pop's melted. Need a new one,' he laughed. 'Then park, yeah?'

'Nah, not me,' Nathan said. 'I'm gonna go and see Megan, catch me some rays in her back garden ... maybe more ... before her mum gets back from work.'

Jake and I were staring at him.

'What?' He laughed.

'You should be revising, not shagging,' I said doing an impression of his dad's voice. 'Study leave starts in just four days, young man, and if you don't get forty GCSEs and bring us home the blood of a nun in a gold-plated vial, we will be restricting your pocket money for the rest of your life.'

'You're an idiot,' Jake said, laughing and punching my arm.

'You sound well like my dad and that's freaky,' Nathan said with his eyes wide. 'Anyways, gotta dash, gotta get me some class-A Megan lovin'.' He straightened up his bag and started walking off.

'Nath,' Jake shouted after him.

Nathan turned around, but carried on walking backwards.

'Remember, don't be silly, wrap your willy,' he shouted, so loudly that a few of the old ladies at the bus stop tutted and gave him really dirty looks.

Nathan turned around and walked off, giving us the middle finger as he went.

'So, do you reckon he's tapped her yet then, or do you think he's all mouth?' Jake asked me. He grabbed a handful of my cold chips and leant back on the bench, squinting from the sun.

We were sitting in our usual spot on the bench in the park halfway between mine and Jake's. It was pretty much where we always went when we were out. It had sort of become our bench. We liked it. It gave us a good view of everything that was going on while we sat there and chatted or whatever.

'Who? Nathan and Megs? Doubt it, he's all mouth,' I said.

'I dunno,' Jake said. 'I haven't seen him pick up a book in weeks.'

'Doesn't mean he's done it.'

Jake sat up straight and turned to me. 'Have you not seen how confident he's got lately? He's gone from shy, skinny, little mummy-and-daddy-pleasing geek who froze up whenever a whiff of titty walked by, to cocky, confident maybe a little bit mouthy on occasions. It's a textbook symptom of virginity losing.'

'Maybe he's just happy he's got a girlfriend,' I said.

'Why are you so uncomfortable with it?'

'I guess I never thought he'd be first, you know ...'

'Why not?'

'Because he used to freeze up when a whiff of titty walked past.'

'Don't be using my expressions, Ads.' Jake punched me in the arm. 'Don't worry, we'll find you some.'

'Er yeah, don't forget you're as far away from finding some as I am. Same boat my friend, same boat,' I said.

Jake shook his head. 'Look over there,' he said. 'That's my dream girl.'

In the distance, four girls were walking towards us.

'Kelly Dawson?' I asked. The sun was in my eyes so I couldn't quite make her out.

'Oh yes,' Jake said. 'Man, what I'd do to that.'

'You've got no chance.' I laughed at how outrageous he was.

'Looks like they're heading this way,' Jake said. There was a half-smile on his face, but his eyes said he was as confused as I was. They were definitely walking towards us, though. Definitely.

'Holy shit,' Jake said, sitting up straight. 'Look at them with

57

their ties off and their buttons all undone and their skirts hitched up – God bless this heat wave.'

'Down, boy,' I said.

They were definitely walking towards us and I wondered why. They were probably bored or something and wanted to come and take the piss out of us to pass the time.

'Gissa chip,' Kelly said when she got to the bench. All I could stare at were her tits, which were massive and poking right out her shirt.

'We're just going over the shop. Want anything?' One of her mates asked her.

'I've got everything I want right here,' she said. She was looking straight at Jake with a really sexy smile. I couldn't believe it.

He slid across the bench, barging me out the way. 'Sit down, beautiful,' he said. I almost choked on my chip.

He put his arm around her. 'You're looking really sexy today, baby. What can Jake do for you?'

'I saw what happened back there, you know, with Adam and his trainers. Man, that was well harsh. Those boys are right twats,' she said.

'I see,' Jake said. 'They are; very, very twatty,' he said. He was looking straight at her tits.

'I was standing by the other bus stop, on the corner,' she said. 'I saw you climb up into the tree to get Adam's trainers back...'

'You did?'

'Yeah,' she said, her voice getting sexier. 'You're a proper hero, Jake,' she said.

It was comedy gold. I wish I had thought to record it. Kelly Dawson coming on to Jake? Pretty much every boy in our year wanted to tap that girl. She never gave it out to anyone. Made out like she was a proper saint and that. It had to be a wind up.

I was trying so hard not to laugh.

'I know,' Jake said. 'That's just what friends do.'

'There's a film on I quite want to see, you know,' she said to him.

I gasped. It wasn't a wind-up. Him climbing up that effing

tree to get my stupid no-name trainers down, which, quite frankly, really stank and could have done with being incinerated, made Kelly Dawson fall in love with him. Or just want to shag him. But even that was a miracle in itself, owing to the fact she was all virginal and stuff.

It could have gone either way for Jake, depending on what his next line was. I braced myself for it.

'I can take you if you like?' He said. It was short. It was sharp. It was straight to the point. He sounded like he was about to choke on his own words, probably in disbelief at the situation, but he'd done it.

'Saturday? The day after we break up for study leave?' She asked.

'Yeah, babes, I can do that,' he said.

'Add me on Facebook, yeah? I'll inbox you my number,' she said, standing up. She smiled and walked over to her friends and Jake leant back all cool. He blew her a kiss and she giggled.

As soon as they were out of our eye line, he grabbed my arm so tight, and put his face right up close to mine, and squealed like he was five again.

'Oh my fucking God, Adam. Oh my God, did you see her tits?'

'I did see her tits,' I said, but he wasn't listening.

'Fuck me, oh my God, oh my God,' he said. 'I'm going out with Kelly fucking Dawson.' He was bouncing around so much that you would have been forgiven for thinking he'd just eaten his entire body weight in Skittles and was on a huge sugar rush.

'I know you are,' I said.

'Let's go,' he said.

'Where?' I asked.

'I dunno, let's go and celebrate, innit. We can go round Meg's and tell Nath,' he jumped up off the bench and bounced off towards the park gate giving me no choice but to follow him.

We were back in Jake's kitchen after Nathan had told us firmly to piss off and leave him and Megan to it. We'd told Debbie and she was hopping from one foot to the other with excitement.

'Is she pretty?' She asked. 'Get her up on Facebook; I want to see what she looks like.'

'Mum, please,' Jake said.

We helped ourselves to an orange juice lolly out the freezer and were sitting at the table while Debbie emptied the contents of her purse out.

'Mum, serious?' Jake asked, looking at all the coins all over the place.

'Yes Jake, that's all I've got until Monday,'

'I can't go on a date with a score worth of pounds and fifty pees. She's gonna think I'm a right cheapskate,' he said.

'Change it up down the shop, then,' Debbie said, counting it out.

Jake stood up. 'Right, let's go check out my threads,' he said to me. 'I gotta make sure I look reem.'

'You've got four days yet. You don't need to choose your clothes now,' I said following him out the kitchen.

'Yeah, true dat. Let's go play Xbox then,' he said.

For the next four days Jake and Kelly did nothing but flirt at school. They were so sickly sweet and disgusting, it made me want to throw up all over them. Then we broke up for the summer – apart from exams, but in our head they didn't really count – and it was the day of Jake's date with Kelly.

I walked him down to the corner, calming his nerves and trying not to choke on all the Lynx he'd doused himself in. When we got there, I gave him a man hug and told him good luck. That was the last time I saw him for three whole days straight.

I sat and festered. I watched Storage Wars and episodes of Come Dine with Me. I played a bit of guitar and slept, lots. Most of all, I lay in bed, checking my texts, Facebook, and Twitter for any signs of life from Jake or Nathan but there was nothing. They were both loved up and I was abandoned. I was confined to my flea pit of a bedroom with only my TV for company.

I was bored and I was hot.

And I was properly pissed off with both of them.

On the Monday morning, I'd had enough, so I had a shower for the first time in days, then I made my way round to Jake's. I knew that his big, lazy arse would no way be out of bed that early. I was going to swoop in, jump on his head and claim him as mine for the day, before he could get to his phone and piss off out with Kelly.

I knocked on the door four times. There was no sign of life from his house. I reckoned Debbie was out shopping or something and Jake was still in bed snoring his head off.

'Jake,' I shouted.

I sat on the doorstep for a bit then wondered what the point was, so I walked over to Nathan's to see if he was in.

He answered the door in his boxers. His hair was all fluffy and pre-gel perfection ritual.

'Morning,' I said, and barged past him into the hallway.

'Ad, man, I got Megs upstairs, know what I mean?'

'Whoa, I'm surprised you remembered my name,' I said.

'Where's Jake?' Nathan asked. 'Go round and bug him instead. I'm getting down, man. Got her waiting up there, man, she's–'

'You two can't abandon me, it's not right.'

'We're not abandoning you.'

'Yeah, you are.'

'No, we're not.' He paused and looked up the stairs. 'Look, lemme go back up and see her. I'll text you in a bit. We'll go park later, yeah?'

'Fine,' I said. 'He's got chlamydia,' I shouted up the stairs, before walking out his front door.

'You're a wanker,' he laughed, and shut the door behind me.

Back at Jake's, I knocked once, and Debbie let me in.

'Morning, sweetheart,' she said.

'Is he in bed?' I followed her down the hallway into the kitchen where she was unpacking the shopping.

'No, he's not actually. Has he not texted you?'

'Not in three days,'

'Oh, new love, eh?' She laughed. She opened a multi-pack of crisps and handed me a packet. 'Juice?' She asked, opening a carton of orange.

'So is he with her?' I asked.

'He stayed there last night,' she winked.

I got a glass out the cupboard, poured some juice, and tried to take it all in.

'You do know you can still stay here whenever you like, don't you? Even if he's not here – this is your home, too.'

I shrugged. It didn't feel right being there without him.

'I'll get him to call you when he gets in,' she said, with her head cocked to the side and her bottom lip out in sympathy.

I had no choice but to go back to my bedroom, on my own, and sulk. Both of them had a girlfriend and I had nothing. It was meant to be the best summer ever, but I was on my own.

Neither of them called me later that day. It didn't matter how many times I checked my phone, how many indirect status updates I posted, there were no missed calls, no texts, nothing. I'd been abandoned.

About half seven, I checked Facebook again and saw that they'd both tagged themselves at the park with Kelly and Megan. 'Double date' it said. I was gutted. I looked around my four walls, at the sun trying to come through my thin little curtain and at my tiny TV. That was my life. That was how I was going to spend my summer. No friends, no family, nothing.

I was so pissed off with them both; I shoved my feet in my smelly, no-name trainers and marched down the park. But by the time I got there, they'd gone.

I decided there and then that I was never going to speak to either of them again.

I un-friended them both on Facebook and deleted their numbers. They didn't need me anymore, so I didn't need them.

I woke up the next morning when a stone hit my bedroom window, cracking the glass. I jumped out of bed, opened it and put my head out.

Jake's eyes were so wide they were almost popping out of his head and Nathan's hand was over his mouth.

'Nathan, you idiot,' Jake shoved him hard.

He'd broken my window. 'What the–?'

'Let us in,' Nathan shouted up.

'What am I meant to tell my dad?' I shouted down.

'Tell him a pigeon flew into it,' Nathan said, trying not to laugh.

I clocked Mrs Henderson in her front garden next door, pruning her roses or whatever it was she was doing. She was trying to pretend she wasn't paying attention, but I knew she was, so I had to go downstairs and talk to them, even though I didn't want to. They weren't going to go away.

When I opened the front door, Jake was telling Nathan he was going to have to get his mum and dad to pay for the window. Nathan was saying he couldn't because they'd go mental at him.

'I don't care,' I said. 'You just smashed my window. If you don't tell them, I will.'

'Who's rattled your virginal cage?' Nathan asked.

'Gonna let us in?' Jake asked.

'Nope,' I said.

'Go on?'

'Nope.'

'Please?'

'Nope.'

'Adam, for fuck's sake, let us in,' Nathan shouted.

'Piss off,' I said. I pushed the door shut but Jake put his big lanky foot in it. They both used all their weight to push it and I was no match for them.

'Can't you just piss off?' I said as the door flew back open and they walked in.

'What's with the un-friending on Facebook?' Jake asked. His face was serious as he marched straight into the kitchen and checked the kettle for water.

'What's with the acting like I don't exist?'

'We're not acting like you don't exist. You'll understand when you get a girlfriend of your own,' Nathan said.

'Nath, man, I said keep your mouth shut and let me do the talking,' Jake said. He put the kettle on and got three mugs out the cupboard, checking to see if they were clean before putting tea bags in.

'You're well upset, aren't you?' He gave me a sideways

glance while counting out the sugars. Nathan sat up on the work surface; looking offended that he'd been told to keep his mouth shut.

'Wouldn't you be?' I asked him.

'Nah, not really–'

'Nathan, shut the fuck up,' Jake said. 'We're sorry, man, we didn't think.'

'Doesn't matter now,' I said. I folded my arms and leant against the door frame.

'Why's that?' Jake asked.

'Because we're not friends anymore.'

I went to walk away but my joggers and boxers were being pulled down and before I could do anything about it, Jake's big hand slapped my right arse cheek so hard that I buckled under the stinging pain.

'Jake, you twat,' I punched him in the arm and pulled my trousers back up.

He flashed me his cheesiest grin.

'I hate you,' I said, but I was trying not to smile.

Nathan jumped down off the side and put five twenty-pound notes on the table. 'Then you won't want to come with us today then, will you?'

'Where did you get that?' I asked.

'Le bank of le mum and le dad,' he said smugly. 'Even though I still don't think we've got anything to be sorry for, consider it an apology.'

We all stood looking at the money on the table. It was guilt money from Nathan's parents. They were never there. Their idea of showing him love and attention came in the form of crisp, twenty-pound notes. Not that Nathan ever complained.

'Where we going, then?'

Jake handed me a mug of tea the exact colour I like it.

'Nowhere with you,' Nathan said. 'We're not friends anymore, remember?'

'You shut up and drink your tea,' Jake said and handed him his mug. 'And you shut up and drink your tea,' he said to me. 'And I'm gonna drink my tea, and when we've all finished drinking; and Adam's got his, quite frankly, cheesy-smelling arse into the shower and dressed, we're hopping on the train to the seaside for the day, to blow that lot on the pier.'

'You serious?' I asked.

'Hell yeah, we're serious,' Nathan said, smiling.

'No girls?'

'Not a whiff of pussy in sight,' Jake said.

'We're sorry.' Nathan said. His bottom lip was poking out.

Jake fluttered his eyelashes at me. 'Are we forgiven?'

I picked up the twenties from the table. My stomach was doing a dance. 'Yeah, go on then,' I said, rolling my eyes and doing a big exaggerated sigh.

'Excellent,' Jake said. 'Now gimme your phone.'

'Why?'

''Cause while you wash your ball sack in the shower, I'm gonna re-add us on Facebook,' he said.

'Don't ever be knobbish again?' I asked them both.

'Likewise, douchebag,' Nathan said.

We were in year twelve when we went back to school and A-Levels were a massive shock. We had to knuckle down and work so hard that there wasn't a lot of time for much else.

The autumn term always goes quickest. One minute, it's the first day back; and then in a flash, it's Halloween, then Fireworks' Night, then it's December, and we're eating advent calendar chocolates after our Coco Pops in the morning, and then... Well then, it was Ed's fancy dress party. The night we met Danny. The night everything changed, and I can't write about that. Not yet. I'm not ready. I can't, because that night was the beginning of the end for us three.

So I'm going to have to leave it here.

Seven

It turned out that Josie had the raging hump with me for bailing on our game of pool and hot chocolate the night before.

I knew she had the raging hump with me because she didn't sit with me at breakfast; she didn't look at me all through our group therapy session, and didn't ask me to go down with her for a cigarette afterwards.

It was like I didn't exist.

Normally, I'd have gone into panic overdrive, avoiding her as much as I could, while being terrified she'd confront me and make me feel awful about myself. Now, I didn't really care too much. Not in a defensive way or anything, I just didn't feel anything about it. I had no emotions at all.

David had come in to see me after group therapy and told me he'd read everything I'd written so far and it was great. He didn't say anything else. He definitely didn't tell me he didn't think I was crazy after all, and he was going to let me go home, like I'd hoped.

I wanted out.

I wasn't crazy or mad or insane. I just didn't want to live anymore.

It was my right, whether I lived or died. It wasn't up to them to decide. It wasn't up to them, or my dad, or anyone else who thought it would be a genius idea chucking me in this crazy place so I could get 'better'.

They weren't going to be able to make me better.

I sat on my bed when I should have been downstairs with Josie having a fake fag, trying to get my brain to work out ways I could either get out, or end my life while I was here.

My brain wouldn't work, so I got my pad out, turned to a new page, and I wrote a list.

Ways to get out

1. *Try and find out the keycode to the ward door and the outside door. (This will mean sorting things out with Josie so I can watch and try and memorise when we go outside for fags.)*
2. *When outside for a fake fag, just bolt it. Run. Run really fast. (This will also mean sorting things out with Josie.*
3. *Find a window with no bars on it (nurses' kitchen?) and climb out.*

Ways to kill myself in here

1. *Find something sharp and slit both my wrists while in the toilet. (Will have to do it quickly.)*
2. *Try and sneak to the nurses' station when nobody's there and grab the keys for the cleaners' store at the end of the corridor and drink loads of bleach. Or wait for the cleaners to come and just grab some and drink it really quickly, while the cupboard is open.*
3. *Save up all my pills and take them all at once. (Work out how to hide them in mouth for when they ask you to open to make sure you've taken them and work out where to hide them.)*

Out of all of those, I reckoned bolting it while outside on a fag break, or breaking into the cleaners' cupboard and drinking all the bleach would be my best options. I just had to work out which one, and when to do it.

I put the pad down and wondered about Debbie and Polly. I knew it'd only been the day before yesterday that David said he was going to call them but, if they were going to come, they'd have come in as soon as they heard.

Which meant they weren't coming. Debbie still hated me, and the fact Polly found me half-dead on the landing probably finally tipped her over the edge into never wanting to see me again.

I was totally on my own.

It didn't matter though, because I had a solid plan and I'd make it work by the end of the day.

'Adam,' Damian's head poked round my door. 'Fancy coming and doing some music therapy?'

I stared at him, wondering what the hell music therapy was.

'Oh, come on, it's actually alright,' he said.

I shook my head. I needed to keep an eye out for the cleaners.

He came in and sat on my bed. 'Did David tell you about the privileges system?'

I shook my head.

'Do this and I'll put you down for privileges. Some of them can be things like having one of us get you your favourite takeaway, maybe even letting you come with us to get it.'

I sat up straight. That sounded like an option. I needed an option in case I couldn't get to the bleach. If I got out of here to go to get a takeaway, I could definitely bolt it and run away.

'You coming then?'

I was. But I was still going to keep an eye out for the cleaners.

Music therapy was with a woman who came in once a week, and was properly trained in it. We sat in a circle and she played a song, some sort of classical music, and asked everyone how they felt about it. Then she asked everyone to choose an instrument out of the box, there were triangles, tambourines and little drums and stuff. It was like being back in a music lesson in primary school, except it all kicked off when Blake took the drum Caitlin wanted and refused to swap.

They had a huge row which the music-therapy woman couldn't control. It only ended when Caitlin smacked Blake round the back of the head with the drum stick, and was pulled out of the room kicking and screaming by one of the nurses.

We were told we had some free time until dinner and were sent off.

I was going to sit in view of the cleaning cupboard at the end of the corridor and bide my time.

As we walked out of the therapy room, Damian was leaning against the nurses' station.

'You two,' he said, pointing at me, then Josie.

She looked at me then looked at the floor.

'You fallen out?' Damian asked.

Josie shrugged.

'Wanna tell me what happened?' He asked.

Neither of us spoke.

'Sure?'

She gave a big sigh. 'Adam just fucked off and left me like a loser by the pool table yesterday. He was meant to be getting hot chocolate but he just disappeared. When I asked everyone if they'd seen him, Blake said he was back in his room,' Josie said.

'How did that make you feel?' Damian asked. He motioned for us to go and sit down on the chairs at the side of the nurses' station.

'Like crap, actually,' Josie said, sitting down next to Damian. I chose to stand.

'Why did it make you feel like that?' Damian asked her.

'Because I was just trying to be his friend, you know. Make him feel welcome and stuff. There was no need to be treated like that,' she said.

'Do you remember the chat we had about trying not to take things personally?' Damian asked her.

70

'Yeah, but …'

'Maybe Adam just needed some time alone, and he can't articulate his feelings, can he?'

'Did you just want time alone?' Josie looked up at me.

I nodded.

'There you go,' Damian said. 'I know that what he did might have seemed rude, but try to think about how hard it must be for Adam at the moment. He can't speak to tell us what he needs or wants; just try to bear that in mind?'

'I'm sorry,' she whispered.

'So are you friends again?' Damian asked.

Josie stood up and moved towards me and before I could stop her, she'd wrapped her skinny arms around my neck and hugged me hard while I froze to the spot.

'I just want him to be OK,' she said to Damian as she pulled away.

'I know you do, Jose, but you got to remember that you can't fix everything,' he said.

'Wanna go and get that hot chocolate?' Josie asked.

I didn't. I didn't understand why she cared about me. She didn't seem to care about any of the others, so why me? It made me suspicious, especially because she knew about what happened that night. Also, I didn't need a friend. It wasn't what I wanted. What I wanted was to watch the cleaning cupboard. But I didn't have a choice. I had to be good in case I couldn't get to the cleaning cupboard and getting out on privileges was my only option. Hot chocolate it was.

Later, after dinner, Josie came to my room. She said she thought I might want some company (I didn't) and she sat on my bed telling me all about the others and what was wrong with them.

I still hadn't seen the cleaners and I was wondering if they came late at night. I really wanted to be keeping my eye out for them, but I couldn't concentrate on watching my doorway in case they walked past because Josie was commanding all of my attention.

That was when I made the impulsive decision to let her in on my plan. I thought she might be able to help.

I opened the notebook at the page of my list and I showed her.

At first, she smiled, maybe thinking it was going to be something good, or funny. But as she read, her face dropped. When she finished she closed the book and looked up at me, shocked.

Then she got up and walked out of my room without saying another word.

I knew then that I'd made a massive mistake.

Eight

I was on code red alert suicide watch. I was to be constantly supervised, twenty-four hours a day. A nurse was all but handcuffed to my side, when I slept, when I woke up, when I ate breakfast, even when I went to the loo. It was humiliating.

If Josie thought she could be my friend now, she could get lost. She'd betrayed me. She'd gone straight up to the night nurse and told them what was in my pad and it all went mental.

'I'm sorry,' she'd said crying. 'I did it because I care.'

I shouldn't have trusted her and I was cross at myself for letting her close.

Owing to my new suicide risk tag, I was seeing David twice a day.

He was sitting on a chair, by my bed, and he was clicking his pen over and over again while reading from my notepad.

'You can leave,' he said to the nurse who automatically did as she was told, no questions or sighs or anything at all.

We were alone.

'I'm confused, Adam,' he said.

I sat up.

'I've read everything in your notebook, all the stuff you've written for me about Jake and Nathan and it's good, it's really good stuff. I'm pleased.' He flipped a few pages back and forward. 'The last thing you wrote was that you were going to have to stop and not go into what happened at the Christmas party, right?'

I nodded.

'And then the next thing in your notebook is your grand, master escape-or-kill-yourself plan. Are they connected? I mean, did thinking about the Christmas party make you have suicidal thoughts again?'

I shrugged.

'So the suicidal thoughts have been there the whole time?'

I didn't want to admit to it. I didn't want him to know that I was just there, behaving myself and biding my time.

'Right,' David said. He tore out the pages of my plan from my notebook and slipped them into his.

'I need you to try your hardest to commit yourself to your recovery, Adam,' he said.

He closed his notebook and looked at me intently.

'I know that right now, it seems like nothing is ever going to get better, but the thing is, you're not going to be able to end your life while you're in here, and I'm not going to let you out until I'm certain you are no longer suicidal.'

He sat forward.

I looked everywhere but at him. I knew what was coming next. I didn't want to hear it.

'I want you to try and tell me what happened at that Christmas party. I'm really intrigued,' he put the notebook on my bed and stood up. 'No more, nothing more at the moment, unless you can.'

I didn't know if I could do any of it, even the Christmas party. I was terrified that thinking about it was going to send me spiralling down into that place again.

'Try and tell me what happened. Let me help you?' David asked.

I lay back down and faced the wall.

He called the nurse in and left me there, trying to block out the thoughts that were already invading my mind. It started at the Christmas party. It was one of those: if we hadn't gone, Jake would still be alive. There was no doubt about it.

'Fuck me, you lot are keen, it's only half seven.' Ed Watkins looked up from where he was emptying bags of ice into a paddling pool full of water.

'It starts at half seven,' I said, confused. The garden was as empty as the house was.

'Never get here for the time it starts, Ad,' he laughed. 'How d'ya get in anyway?'

'Door was on the latch,' Jake said. He grabbed a bag of ice, ripped it open, and emptied it into the pool.

'Cheers, man,' Ed saluted Jake. He turned to me and Nathan. 'Hey, you two don't have to just stand there you know, grab some of those beers and chuck them in.'

I liked Ed. He was all right. He was in year thirteen, the year above us, and he was popular because all the girls fancied him, and that made him cool. We were excited to be invited to his party. Ed had been promising this party since Halloween, but his parents had kept cancelling their weekend away.

'So you finally got rid of your parents?' Nathan asked.

'Yeah, they've gone to some posh hotel for the weekend for Dad's Christmas work do. Thanks for wearing your costumes, anyway. Feels a bit odd now it's not Halloween anymore, right?'

'I like yours. It's funny 'cause it's ironic.' Jake pointed to Ed's outfit. He was dressed as a vampire.

'My name is Edward, couldn't not, really, could I?'

'So who's gonna be your Bella then?' I asked. Nathan elbowed me in the ribs and I scolded myself for sounding stupid.

Ed laughed. 'I've got my eye on Jessica in your year. She's friends with your Kelly, right?' He asked Jake.

'Jessica Terry?' Jake asked.

'Yep, she's got amazing tits, hasn't she?' Ed asked. He ripped open a box of beer and started chucking the cans in the pool of ice, one by one. 'They're definitely coming, right?'

'Yeah, man, they went out earlier to get their costumes and shit,' Jake said.

'What they coming as?' Ed threw Jake and Nathan a beer each. He nodded to me to take one myself. I didn't really like beer, but I didn't want to look like an idiot so I took one.

'Dunno,' Jake said, shrugging. 'She tried telling me but I was right in the middle of a game of Call of Duty at the time, so I may have not been listening properly.'

'Girls, man.' Ed rolled his eyes. 'How's things with Megan?' he asked Nathan.

'Yeah, she's amazing,' Nathan said.

'Look at you, you're well loved-up,' Ed said.

Nathan smiled. 'Might be.'

'Totally,' Ed laughed. 'Adam, you got a girlfriend?' He asked.

'Nope,' I said and looked straight at the floor. I didn't have a girlfriend, wasn't even close. I was as pure as they came and totally embarrassed about it.

Ed stood up straight and eyed me up and down. 'Jake's a mummy, right, obvious. Nath's Superman, even more obvious.' He cocked his head to the side. 'But, seriously dude, why the fuck are you dressed as an old man? I mean, I know you're a bit weird and shit, but–'

'I'm Albert Einstein,' I said. Jake and Nathan were looking at each other, trying not to piss themselves laughing. It'd been a running joke since the costume was delivered. They reckoned nobody would know what I was dressed as, but I said everyone knew who Einstein was.

'It's meant to be ironic,' Nath said through his snorts.

'Why's that?' Ed asked.

''Cause he's a swot, innit,' Jake said. 'Einstein was clever. Adam's proper clever, too.'

'Riiiiiight,' Ed said looking at Jake.

'He reckons he'll pull if the girls think he's clever,' Nathan said.

'While dressed as an old man?' Ed asked. 'Yeah, 'cause all the girls wanna sleep with an old man.' He laughed.

'Oi, you're all bitches,' I said and opened the beer I didn't want to drink.

'It's alright, Ad, we'll find you someone,' Ed said. His eye line went to the girl walking out into the back garden dressed as a cheerleader. 'But not her,' he said. 'That's my sister, strictly

76

hands off.'

'Where's the vodka?' She asked Ed.

'No, no way,' Ed said. 'You're sixteen, Polly. No vodka, I've told you that.'

'I don't give a fuck what you've told me, I'll drink what I want,' she said.

We all stood wide eyed, our mouths open.

'And what the fuck are you lot looking at?' She asked.

'If you want it, you'll have to find it yourself, and if Mum and Dad go bat shit when they get back, I had nothing to do with it,' Ed told her.

'Get fucked,' she said, walking back inside with her middle finger up.

Ed rolled his eyes at her. 'Right boys,' he said. He rubbed his hands together and smiled. 'Let's get this party started.'

Jake had gone off with Kelly as soon as she'd got there, on account of the fact she was dressed as Catwoman with her tits half hanging out. 'I need to spend some time alone with her, guys, you know what I mean?' He'd said to us before patting me on the back and disappearing with her into the party.

Nathan and I were in the kitchen. Every time someone walked into the room, his head darted around. He was waiting for Megan. I was hoping she wouldn't show because if she did, he'd go off with her and I'd be left like a loner.

'Have this,' he said, handing me a plastic shot glass with bright green liquid in it.

'What is it?'

'Fuck knows,' he said. 'Just drink it.'

'I dunno what it is.'

'Stop being a pussy and drink it,' he said, holding his glass up. 'Ready? One ... two ... three ...'

We downed them. It burnt the back of my throat and down my food pipe all the way to my stomach.

'That was disgusting,' I said, through my screwed up face.

Nathan laughed.

A strange atmosphere came over the kitchen. Like it'd had gone a bit quiet and really tense. All eyes were on the group of people who were walking through like they owned the place. They weren't in costume, and they didn't look friendly.

'Who are they?' I asked Nathan.

'Dunno,' he said, watching them walk out into the back garden.

'That's Ed's cousin, Danny, and his mates, they're proper twats, just stay away from them,' Megan's voice came from behind Nathan. His face lit up, he spun around, wrapped his arms around her and gave her a kiss.

'You made it?'

'Well, yeah,' she said. She pulled away from him. 'You alright, Ads?'

'Yeah,' I said.

'Come on baby, let's get a drink from outside,' Nathan said and took her hand and led her out the back.

Not good. I should have had a sign round my neck with loner written on it. I looked around for someone I knew well enough to talk to until I saw Ed's sister Polly looking at me from the other side of the kitchen. She smiled. I had no idea why she was smiling at me. Either it was sarcastic, or she was bipolar. I looked away.

'Alright? What's the matter?' A girl bumped into me as she walked past to get to the sink.

'Me?' I asked.

'Yeah, you,' she slurred. She was clearly drunk.

She filled up her plastic cup with ice from the sink, then took a bottle of Jack Daniels from the side and filled it up over halfway, then added some Coke.

'Do you want some Coke with that JD?' I asked.

She put the bottle back on the side and gave me a filthy look.

'Sorry,' I said. I scanned her up and down while trying to hide the fact I was checking her out. Schoolgirl's outfit. Standard lazy girl's fancy dress costume. Blonde hair in pigtails. Not fat, but not skinny. OK really. Nice-ish tits but not as nice as Kelly's – Jake could have that one.

'Britney Spears,' she said.

'Britney Spears?'

'Yeah, not just a schoolgirl, I'm Britney Spears.'

78

'She's a bit outdated now, isn't she?' I asked.

Silence, and then another filthy look. I should probably never talk to girls, ever. I was crap at it. I was coming across like a total idiot.

'You can't talk, you're dressed as an old man,' she said. 'Who the fuck comes to a fancy dress party dressed as an old man?' She asked.

Nice come back.

'I'm Albert Einstein,' I said.

She took a sip of her drink and leant against the sink to stop herself swaying. 'Is he the one who invented gravity?' She asked.

'Nobody invented gravity. Gravity just is,' I said.

'Yeah, you know who I mean,' she leant over and grabbed my arm and stumbled a bit. 'The guy who sat under the tree and the apple fell on his head?'

'Newton?'

'No, he invented the light bulb,' she said.

'No, Edison invented the light bulb,' I said.

'Who's Edison?' She asked.

I heard a sarcastic snort and looked up to find Polly watching us both with a huge smirk on her face. In her hand she was holding that elusive bottle of vodka.

'Edison invented gravity?' Britney Spears asked me.

'Fuck me, you were last in the queue when they were handing out the brains, weren't you?' Polly said to Britney, who curled up her nose.

'Thomas Edison invented the light bulb,' Polly said to her. 'Newton came up with the theory of gravity after an apple fell on his head, and Einstein and I are going upstairs for a drink,' she said.

I was stunned at how smooth that was and, before I could argue, she grabbed my hand and took me out of the kitchen, into the hallway, weaving in and out of people, and up the stairs to her room.

'You're welcome,' she said, shutting the door and flinging herself onto her bed.

Her room was all lava lamps, dream catchers, and incense

79

sticks. Total hippy paradise. Cosy though, and at least I wasn't on my own anymore, but...

'What?' She asked.

'If Ed knows I'm in here with you, he's going to rip my balls off,' I said.

'Fuck Ed, come and sit down,' she smiled.

'Are you going to try and shag me?' I asked.

'Only if you want me to,' she said.

She was sitting on the bed with her legs crossed, so I could see her knickers under her cheerleader's skirt. She was too busy leaning back against the wall and rolling a fag to notice me looking, or twig that I now had a massive boner.

I sat down on the edge of her bed so she couldn't see it.

'Want one?' She asked, without looking up.

'I don't smoke,' I said.

I'd seen Polly around school a couple of times, but I hadn't realised she was Ed's sister. I hadn't ever paid any attention to her, but sitting in her room, right next to her, I realised how pretty she was. When she tucked her long hair behind her ear, I actually wanted to lean over and kiss her.

'Bollocks,' she said.

'What?' I laughed. She may have been pretty, but she was no lady.

She leant over the side of the bed and was rooting around under it, which meant that her really crisp white knickers and her arse were on show and it was pretty much perfect and cute.

She got back up holding a pack of filters.

'Help yourself,' she said, pointing at the vodka.

I wasn't falling into that trap. I'd end up drunk, then she'd take advantage of me. OK, I really wanted to shag her but there were three reasons I didn't think it was right: we weren't together or anything and I'd never done it before; she was a bit of a demon and I was quite intimidated by her; and Ed would rip my balls off, pickle them in a jar and take them to school, where everyone would laugh at me even more than they already did.

'Adam,' she said. 'Vodka, get it.'

'What we got to do with it?'

She snorted, grabbed the bottle and took a swig of it straight. Like swigging vodka from a bottle was the most natural thing in the world. She handed it to me.

I didn't want to look like a massive idiot, so I took a swig myself. I nearly choked to death.

'You're alright, you know.' She laughed at me and went over to the window.

I took another swig. It wasn't as bad but it was still disgusting.

'I mean you're a bit strange, but I like strange,' she said.

She opened the window and lit her cigarette. 'Eugh,' she said, looking at some of the people in the garden. 'Can't stand that wanker.'

'Which one?' I asked, poking my head out.

'That one there. He's our cousin Danny.'

'Yeah, we saw them when they came in. Everyone in the kitchen went quiet. Why don't you like him?'

'He thinks he's hard.'

'Is he bad news then?' I asked.

'No, he just thinks he is. He's harmless really.'

'He's older than us?'

'Yeah, he's twenty-one. He's not in college or anything anymore. My aunt's always moaning about him getting a job and stuff, and how she and my uncle can't keep giving him money all the time.'

'What does he do with himself, then?'

'Just bums around really. Must be so fulfilling,' she said.

'Who's the girl?' I asked her.

'Sarah.'

'Danny's girlfriend?' I asked, but I wasn't listening when she answered. Nathan and Megan were up the end of the garden. They weren't in their usual position with her wrapped round him and him touching her up. They were serious. Her hands were waving about all over the place. He looked like he was about to cry.

'Are you even listening to me?' She asked.

'Do they look like they're having a row?' I nudged my head at where Nathan and Megan were.

We watched them in silence. The only sound was Polly pulling on her cigarette, inhaling, then blowing the smoke out.

'Yeah, looks like it,' she said. 'Is that your mate Nathan?'

'Yeah,' I said.

'That his girlfriend?'

'Yup.'

Nathan's arm reached out for Megan but she shoved him off and walked quickly down the garden. He stood with his hand over his mouth, watching her go.

'Looks serious,' Polly said.

'I better go and see if he's OK,' I said.

'Leave him a minute,' Polly said. 'Let me finish this first. You can keep an eye on him from up here – let him have a minute to himself.'

'He looks pretty upset.'

'He'll be OK,' she said, touching my arm, which made my stomach flip. 'Anyway,' she said. 'Tell me more about ...'

I'd stopped listening again. Nathan had sat down on a bench at the bottom of the garden. His face was in his hands.

'Adam?' Polly said.

'Look.'

'Oh ...'

'I should go and ...'

'He's a big boy, Ads, he can look after himself.' She took a final drag on her cigarette and flicked it out the window. Nathan got up and started walking down the garden, head down. I walked away from the window and towards the door.

'Well I need to find out where Megan is. And Jake,' I said. 'I haven't seen him for ages.'

'Suit yourself,' she said.

'Come with me?' I asked. 'Where are all your friends?'

'None of them are here tonight; Ed wouldn't let me invite them. No year elevens allowed,' she said.

'I'll come back up,' I said, hoping she'd want me to.

'OK,' she smiled and plonked herself back on her bed.

What I really wanted was to find Jake in a corner somewhere with his hand down Kelly's top, and Megan and Nathan making up in another corner. Then I could have gone straight back up to Polly.

I checked every dark corner of the house. I couldn't find either of them anywhere.

The last place to look was the garden. Where that Danny was. No matter what Polly said about him, I was intimidated by him. I really didn't want to go out there, but then I heard Nathan's laugh.

Bingo. He'd be outside with Jake. Definitely.

I weaved past a few people, went out the back door, and did a quick scan to see Nathan sitting at the table with Danny and his mates.

'Ads.' Nathan nodded at me. 'Grab a drink, come join us. This is Danny, Sarah, and Lucy.'

'What happened with Megan?' I asked.

'He don't wanna talk about that, man,' Danny said.

Sarah and Lucy laughed. Sarah was looking at Nathan like she wanted to jump him there and then.

'Grab a drink and come and sit down,' Nathan said.

'Alright,' I said. 'Let me just go and find Jake,' I said.

'Why do you need to go and find Jake?' Nathan asked. 'Just come and sit down, enjoy yourself, let your hair down ... chill.'

'I'll go and find Jake, we can all chill together, you can tell me what happened with Megan and—'

'Didn't you hear me the first time?' Danny asked. 'I said he don't wanna talk about that.'

I took a few steps back and tried to stop my hands from shaking. 'Nath, come and help me find him,' I said. I wanted to get him away from Danny and his mates. Even if Polly reckoned he was harmless, I didn't like him.

'Go and find him yourself,' Danny said. He gave me a filthy look and turned his head away. Nathan was looking at him intently, then he waved his hand at me to tell me to go away, to get on with it.

'Come back when you've found him,' he said. He was staring at me weirdly.

'Nath?'

'Just come back when you've got him,' he said, a bit more

softly.

'What you doing hanging around with this knob cheese?'
Polly appeared behind me.

'Fuck off,' Danny said to her.

'You fuck off,' she said back.

'Don't start, Pol. I swear to God just don't start, alright?'

'Scared I'm gonna embarrass you in front of your mates?'

'Whatever. Just do one, yeah?'

She turned her back on him. We took a few steps away from them, towards the house. 'Just seen Kelly coming out of my mum and dad's room, Jake'll be in there.'

'Cool,' I said.

'What's he doing with that dick head?' She asked, looking over her shoulder at Nathan and Danny.

I shrugged. 'I don't know. He said to go and find Jake and come back out.'

Polly screwed up her face. 'Find Jake, make sure he's OK, leave Nathan to it.'

'Shouldn't I try and get him away from them?' I whispered.

'I told you, Ads, he's harmless really. What's the worst that could happen?'

Nathan was laughing with Sarah, who still looked like she wanted to jump him. I shook my head.

'Sarah's alright, actually. She's quite sweet. God knows why she hangs around with Danny. Look, if he's had a row with Megan, he'll be getting his ego kissed better with Sarah's flirting. Leave him. Let's go and find Jake, make sure he's OK, then we can go back upstairs and have a quiet drink.'

Even though I felt uneasy, I agreed. Polly was right, Nathan looked like he was having an OK time. I didn't want to hang out with Danny. I'd go and find Jake, make sure he was alright, then slip back upstairs with Polly.

'Laters,' Nathan said as I walked back into the house.

'Top of the stairs, first on the left, I'm just going to grab some ice,' Polly said.

I jogged up the stairs and onto the landing.

'Adam,' Kelly pulled my hand away just as I was about to open the bedroom door.

84

'Where's Jake?' I asked. 'Is he in there?'

'No, there's someone else in there now,' she said, but the tone of her voice was off.

'You were just in there,' I said. 'Polly saw you come out.'

'No I wasn't. No she didn't. Who's Polly anyway?' Her hair was all over the place, she'd blatantly just been shagging.

'Yeah, you did,' I said. I put my hand back on the handle. 'Let me in, I need to speak to Jake.'

'He's not in there,' she said, looking at the floor.

'What?'

She stood to the side; I opened the door and went in. There was a bloke sitting on the bed buttoning up his shirt. I had no idea who he was.

'Where's Jake?'

'Who the fuck is Jake?' He looked up at me.

'Her boyfriend,' I pointed at Kelly.

His face fell. 'What?'

'Listen ...' Kelly said, walking into the room.

The bloke stood up. 'You've got a boyfriend?' He asked.

'I just ...' She stopped talking and looked at me.

Then the penny dropped. 'You've been shagging him?' I asked.

She said nothing.

He barged past and out of the room.

'Did you just cheat on Jake?' I asked her.

She looked at the floor, then up at me. 'Please don't tell him, Ad. I'm fucked; we drank two bottles of wine before we left. It just happened. I couldn't find him. I didn't mean it to, I don't ... I'm sorry ... please don't tell him,' she grabbed my arm. 'Please?'

I shook my head at her.

'Adam,' she cried, but I was already gone and out the door and down the stairs.

Polly caught my arm at the bottom of the stairs. 'Someone said he's out front with Megan ... Adam, what's up?'

I ignored her, opened the front door, and stormed out. Polly was close behind me, asking me what was going on.

Jake and Megan were sitting on the wall at the front of the

house. Jake was holding a bottle of wine, which was almost empty. Megan had a half-full glass.

'Jake,' I said.

'Ads,' he put his arm around me. 'I love you, man,' he said.

'You're fucked,' I said, pulling away from him. His breath stank of wine and his eyes were droopy. 'What's going on?'

'What happened, you see,' he said, swaying. 'What happened was ... What happened?' He asked Megan.

'I dumped Nathan,' she said, looking at the floor.

'What?'

'There was a girl out the back garden who kept looking at him and smiling. I was gonna let it go, but then I caught him smiling back. I had a go, he told me to stop being an idiot,' she said. 'I'm sick of his shit lately, Ads. He's not like he was when we first started going out, he's got an attitude now. I love him, but I can't deal with it. The way that girl was looking at him ...'

'Sarah,' Polly said.

'Is that her name?' Megan asked. 'Anyway, I was gonna go home but Jake caught me here on my way out and told me to stay. He said leave Nath for a bit, then go in, and sort it out with him.'

'What were you doing out here? Why weren't you with Kelly?' I asked Jake.

'Funny story,' he said. 'Thing is, I think I'd had a bit tooooo much of le alcoholohlico beveraaaages. I felt sick. Turns out Kelly hates sick, so I came out here for some fresh air and she stayed inside. Shit, I better go and find her, man. She's probably worrying about me.'

Polly looked at me strangely. 'But I just saw her–'

'What have you and Megan been talking about then?' I interrupted Polly with the first thing that came into my head. I shook my head at her. She shrugged at me, confused.

'We were just talking about why T-Rexes have really small arms,' Jake said. He looked me square in the eye and cracked up. Then he pulled his arms up close to his body and did a really bad impression of a T-Rex trying to drink wine straight from the bottle. Out the corner of my eye, Polly was laughing and I had to stop myself from cracking up.

I turned to Megan. 'Why don't you go back in and find Nath?' I asked.

'Leave it, Ads,' Jake said. He put his mouth really close to my ear. 'They'll be OK tomorrow when everyone's sober and nobody's drunk and everybody can do this ...' He started dancing like a robot.

'Jake.' Kelly stood on the front doorstep.

I shook my head at her in disgust. She gave me a pleading look. Jake hadn't noticed her, so I took his arm and walked him a few paces away from Megan and Polly, and out of Kelly's eye line. I had to tell him.

I held his arms to stop his stupid robot dancing.

'What?' He asked. 'Why you so serious?'

I whispered it in his ear.

He pushed me away slightly, then looked at me with his eyebrows squished together. 'Let me get this straight,' he said, rubbing his forehead while swaying on the spot. 'You just caught my girlfriend shagging another bloke?' He said it so loudly, he caught the attention of Megan, and Polly, who was wincing.

'Jake ...'

He grabbed my arms and looked into my eyes. I'd never seen him look so serious. 'You caught my Kelly in bed with another bloke?'

I was bracing myself for the fact he was about to go crazy. Even Megan had backed off a couple of steps.

'Jake ...'

His face changed and he erupted into one of his belly laughs. He bent over and laughed for ages. It wasn't funny. Not even a little bit. When he came back up, he had tears of laughter in his eyes.

'I didn't actually catch them,' I said, because it was the truth. 'But she did admit it and she told me not to tell you and, of course, the first thing I did was come and tell you,' I said.

He cracked up again. I didn't know how he could find it funny.

'Jake?'

He switched and suddenly I was using all my strength to

87

hold him back.

'I'm gonna fucking kill the wanking twatting bastard. Let fucking go of me, Adam. I'm gonna find him and I'm gonna fucking kill him.'

'He's already gone,' Kelly said. She stood by the gate with her head down and her arms crossed over her chest. Her black make-up had run down her face like she'd been crying.

'You bitch,' he spat. 'You fucking bitch.'

She walked up to him and stopped. 'I'm fucked, Jake,' she was swaying on the spot.

'You're dumped,' he said, right up in her face.

'No,' she cried.

'Fucking yes,' he said.

She tried to grab him, but he pushed her off and stormed inside. I was right behind him, leaving Kelly sobbing in Megan's arms.

'Jake, man,' I shouted over the music.

'Leave me,' he said.

'What the fuck is going on?' Nathan said from the bottom of the stairs, where he was sitting with Sarah. The front door had shut behind us, so at least Megan couldn't see.

'Kelly and Jake are over,' I said.

'What?' He stood up, a bit shocked.

'Who gives a fuck?' Danny said, appearing behind me. 'Come on, we're going,' he said to Sarah and Nathan. Sarah got up and took Nathan's hand and they all walked out the front door.

'What? Where you going?' I asked.

'Away from this shit-hole,' Danny said.

'Hang on, Nath. Nathan, did you hear what just happened? You can't bail. Jake is in a right state,' I said.

'He'll be OK,' he said.

I followed him up the path towards the gate. 'Nath? And what about Megan? What the fuck is going on?'

Megan looked at Nathan holding Sarah's hand with wide eyes. She pushed Kelly away and took a few steps towards Nathan, but Danny put his arm out.

'Know when to leave it,' he said to her.

'Nathan, Jake is in a right state. You can't bail now, he needs us,' I said.

Danny unlocked his car and Nathan and Sarah climbed into the back together. Lucy in the front.

'Nathan,' I said again.

'Fucking leave him,' Danny said. 'He don't wanna hang around with you losers anymore. Especially you,' he pointed at Megan. He got in the car, put the key in the ignition, turned up the music, and sped off down the road. And all we could do was stand there and watch.

Jake was in a right mess, so Polly and I dragged him out of the party – ignoring Kelly, who was begging him – and went straight to the park. Polly said we needed a bit of R&R, away from all the madness.

The plan was to sit on our bench and get absolutely smashed to forget what a bad night it'd been. Actually, that was Jake and Polly's plan. I just went along with it. I let them start on the vodka Polly had brought, while I stayed sober and sensible. Jake was heartbroken. I had to stand guard and make sure our evening didn't get any worse.

'Eugh, it tastes like hairspray,' Jake said and handed the bottle back to Polly. 'Haven't you got anything to go with it?'

'Yeah, cause that was the only thing on my mind as we got you out of there, wasn't it?' She said.

I laughed. She was really good at being sarcastic.

'What you laughing at?' She raised her eyebrow at me but there was a twinkle in her eye. I couldn't help but smile at her.

'Do you two wanna bone each other?' Jake slurred.

'Right, home time,' I said standing up. I didn't trust him not to embarrass me completely in his inebriated state.

'We've only just got here, a-hole,' Jake pulled me back down onto the bench. 'Lighten up a bit. You're so stiff.'

Polly snorted into the vodka bottle.

'You,' Jake said, jabbing her arm. 'You have got a filthy mind, for someone so young.'

'Shut up, I'm only in the year below you.'

'Year eleven?'

'Yeah.'

'So you're fifteen?'

'No, I was sixteen on 3rd September. If I was born a few days earlier, I'd be in your year, and I know for a fact you two are still sixteen, so shut up.'

'I'm seventeen on 2nd January,' Jake said, poking out his tongue at her.

'You're acting like you're four,' she said.

'Just give me that,' Jake said. He grabbed the bottle off her and swigged before pulling a pained face. *'Tastes like hairspray,'* he said again. He got up off the bench and swayed about a bit.

'What you doing, Jake? Sit back down,' I said.

'I'm stretching my legs, man. Leave me alone. Talk to your girlfriend.'

'I can't get over Nathan going off with Danny like that.' I said.

'Danny's an idiot,' Polly said.

'Yeah, I gathered. I just don't get why Nath went off with him.'

'Danny's got this appeal, this charm—'

'Really? I just thought he was an arsehole,' I said.

'Yeah, he is, it's just ...' She looked me straight in the eye. *'It's bothered you, hasn't it?'*

'Of course it's bothered me, look at the state of that,' I pointed at Jake. He was lying in a starfish shape on the grass, singing opera. *'He's our best mate. He should be here right now, not off with some idiot he's just met.'*

'It probably wasn't even Danny,' Polly said. *'It was probably 'cause he fancies that Sarah,'* she said.

'He's got a girlfriend; her name is Megan.'

'Didn't they just have a huge row? Plus, not everyone's as boring as you. He's probably one who likes to dip his toe in all the different puddles before deciding which one he wants to splash about in.'

'Hang on,' I said. *'Did you just call me boring?'*

She smiled. *'Did I say boring? I meant sensible.'*

I rolled my eyes at her.

She put her head on my shoulder and I got a waft of her fruity shampoo right up my nose. It smelt so nice.

'Shall we get him home?' She looked up at me, then back at Jake who was rolling around on the grass. 'He's absolutely fucked.'

I stood up. 'Yeah, but we better take him back to mine. If his mum sees him like this, he's going to be in trouble, and I'll be going down with him.'

'To yours then,' she said.

I didn't have my keys. Couldn't find them anywhere. Jake went mental and then sat on my front doorstep. He was going on and on about how crazy Debbie was going to go when she saw him drunk. He reckoned he'd be grounded for life.

'It's OK,' I said. 'We can sneak you in, gimme your keys,' I said.

'I haven't got them,' he looked up at me. I swear there were tears in his eyes. I didn't blame him; we were going to be in so much trouble.

When we got back, I pushed the doorbell and braced myself. Jake had slumped himself, full weight, against the front door. When Debbie opened it he went flying into the house, and landed flat on his back at her feet.

She looked down at him. Then at Polly. Then she gave me the look she does when she's about to get really cross. I winced and braced myself for it.

'Tell me he's not drunk,' she said. Her tone cut right through me.

'I'm not drunk, Mummy,' Jake said, then he burst out laughing.

There was a pause which felt like a lifetime. 'Help me get him up. Oh my God, you boys, you'll be the death of me, I swear it.'

We helped him to the kitchen table, where he sat down laughing his head off at absolutely nothing. Or something. Whatever it was, I had no idea.

'Sit down,' Debbie said to Polly and me, and she disappeared into the under stairs cupboard. She came out with a huge orange bucket.

'How much has he had?' she asked.

I shrugged.

'Adam.' It was her warning tone.

'I don't know, this thing happened, Kelly went off with this other bloke, and then he got smashed.'

She plonked the bucket on the table. Then made a huge point of sighing.

'I'm sorry,' I said.

She shook her head at me. 'Right then, you two ...'

'I'm Polly,' Polly said to Debbie.

'Hi, Polly,' Debbie smiled then turned back to me. 'You can stay up all night long, and watch him to make sure he doesn't choke on his own vomit in the middle of the night.' She turned to walk out of the kitchen, then stopped and turned back again. 'And if he's sick anywhere but in that bucket, you can clean it up.' She pointed her finger at me, then at Polly, then at Jake who was smiling at her like a crazed maniac.

'Polly, do your parents know where you are?' Debbie asked.

'They're away, but it's OK, I'll text my brother and tell him I'm with Adam. He knows him,' she said.

'Right, I'm going back to bed with ten more grey hairs than when I answered the door,' she said. 'Oh, one sec,' she put her head back through the door. 'Where's Nathan?'

'Don't ask,' I said.

She shrugged and left.

'I love you, Mummy,' Jake called after her.

'I love you too, Jake,' she shouted back, but you could hear the unimpressed tone in her voice.

'I love you too, Mummy,' I called after her.

'I love you too, Adam,' she said. 'But I mean it, stay up, watch him and clean up after him. You boys, honestly.' She disappeared up the stairs.

We put him on the sofa. I ran up really quietly and got his Power Rangers duvet. Polly took the almighty piss out of it, and I made her promise not to tell anyone at school. Which she did. Through the giggles. I put the bucket next to Jake and made him comfortable.

His last words before he passed out were 'Where's Nathan?'
which made me really angry again.

'Have you heard from him?' Polly asked.

I checked my phone. Nothing.

'You can get back now, if you want,' I said to her. 'I'm OK
watching him.'

'Can I have a quick cup of tea before I go?' She asked.

'Are you going to try and shag me?' I asked.

'Haven't we already had this conversation?'

'Yeah but ... Just checking–'

'Well, stop checking and go and make me a cup of tea. Milk,
two sugars, not piss weak.' She smiled. 'I'll stay here and watch
oh he who cannot handle his drink.'

'Polly, we're sixteen – we're not meant to be able to handle
our drink,' I said from the doorway.

'Has anyone ever told you, you sound like an old man
trapped in a teenager's body?' She laughed as I walked away.

When I came back in, she was sitting cross-legged on the
sofa watching Jake. I handed her the tea in my favourite mug.

'You think he's going to be OK?' She asked.

'He's gonna have a raging hangover, but yeah, I think he'll
live,' I said.

'No, I mean about Kelly?'

'I dunno,' I said. His head was poking out the top of the
duvet, his mouth was open slightly, and he was snoring his head
off. He looked restless and I wondered if he was dreaming. I
didn't want him to be heartbroken.

'Does he always snore like that?' Polly was cupping her
mug and blowing on the steam that was rising from the top. Her
hair was hiding half of her face but she was pretty – really,
really pretty. I liked her a lot. She was the first girl I'd liked. I
wondered how I'd not noticed her at school.

'What?' She asked. She was still cupping her mug, her head
didn't move, and neither did her eyes. 'Stop watching me, you
freak.' She turned her eyes a little bit towards me and I saw that
twinkle again.

I couldn't be happy about Polly though, or excited about
what might happen with her. Not while Jake was heartbroken.

That'd be the last thing he'd want to hear, me banging on about Polly when he was devastated about Kelly.

Plus, I shouldn't have gone upstairs with Polly. I should have kept an eye on Jake and Kelly. Made sure they stayed together.

'What you thinking about?' Polly asked, but I didn't want to tell her so I just shook my head.

'Tell me,' she said.

I twisted around and put my feet up on the sofa. 'If I'd stayed with him tonight, I could have made sure Kelly stayed too, then she wouldn't have gone off with that dickhead, and none of this would have happened,' I said.

She raised her eyebrows above the mug as she took a sip. 'How did you draw that conclusion?' She asked.

'I just did,' I said. 'It's true, though.'

'Not really, sometimes shit just happens,' she said. 'Some things are way out of your control. Like the fact Kelly is a slapper ...'

'I just don't want to see him get hurt,' I said. He rolled over to face the back of the sofa.

'You two are really close, aren't you?' She put her mug down and turned to face me. 'Like bromance close?'

'He's family,' I said.

'How come?'

'I've seen him pretty much every day of my life since nursery. My mum worked, Debbie picked us up from school every day. We still sort of do it now, come back here every day, except Debbie doesn't pick us up anymore.'

'That's really close. I wish I had a friend like that,' she said, looking down.

'Since my mum died, I kind of sort of live here anyway because my dad's a massive wanker,' I said. 'Debbie's like my mum now, she's looking after me.'

'When did your mum die?' She asked and it took me aback. Nobody had ever been so upfront about it before; they always do that whole sorry, avoid the subject thing – but Polly, she actually wanted to know about it.

'Two years ago, in a car crash. She walked in on my dad

shagging another woman, and got in the car to drive to the coast to clear her head or something. There was an accident on the way,' I said. I had to take a deep breath. It was the first time I'd said it out loud.

Polly put her hand on mine. She didn't say anything. She didn't have to.

'My dad is still with the woman now,' I said.

Her face screwed up like she was in pain. 'No wonder you practically live here. That's so fucked up, Adam.'

'And Jake was there for me through it all. He held my hand all through Mum's funeral, he fronted up to my dad when he found out about that woman Jackie. He's looked after me through it all. Now do you see why I'm gutted I couldn't stop it happening tonight?' I asked her. I took my hand away and straightened up.

'Yeah,' she said. 'But you just got to do everything you can to be there for him now. That's all you can do,' she said. She leant forwards. For a minute, I thought she was going to kiss me. I pulled back, but all she did was grab my tea from the coffee table and hand it to me. 'Drink,' she said. 'Drink to life being a bitch and there being fuck all you can do about it.' She smiled and all I could look at was that twinkle in her eye.

Polly and I woke the next morning to the sound of Jake heaving his guts up.

'Eugh,' Polly said, screwing her face up and turning away.

I jumped up from where I'd been asleep on the floor and over to him to make sure he was getting it all in the bucket.

'Water,' he gasped.

'On it,' Polly said, running to the kitchen.

When Jake caught his breath, he looked at me, his eyes bloodshot. 'I feel like I've been run over by a stampede of elephants,' he said, then flopped back onto the sofa.

'Here, sip this,' Polly said.

I took the water off her and handed it to him. He gulped it down.

'Bad move, that's gonna come straight back up again,' I said.

'It's cool, man, I'm going back to sleep,' he said. He put the duvet over his head and that was that.

'I'd better get back,' Polly said. She was looking at her phone. 'Ed's been trying to call me for about an hour. He's probably just realised I'm gone.'

'Didn't you text him last night?'

She shook her head.

'What time is it?' I asked.

'Ten past eight,' she said.

'You going to be OK?' I looked at Jake. I couldn't really leave him to walk Polly home.

'Go on.' Debbie appeared at the living room door in her dressing gown. 'Walk her home, I'll keep an eye on the casualty,' she said.

'Thanks, Deb,' I said.

'Hang on, though, you can't go home like that, Polly.' Debbie was looking at Polly's tiny cheerleader's skirt. 'Let me get you some joggers or something.'

'Ads,' Jake's voice came out from under the duvet. 'Do me a favour, get me a bacon sandwich from the café on your way back?'

I looked at Debbie, who rolled her eyes, shook her head, and tutted as she disappeared up the stairs.

'Did you two shag?' Jake asked, his head appearing. 'You best not have while I was in the room,'

'Come on,' I said, ushering Polly out the living room door. I gave Jake an evil look as I followed her.

'Don't forget my sandwich,' he said.

On the way back from Polly's I'd tried calling Nathan, but it was ringing out, then going through to voicemail.

I kept trying through the morning, kept texting him. He was reading my messages and not replying. I was getting more and more wound up with him as the day went on.

Around the afternoon, he'd added three new friends on Facebook: Danny, Sarah, and Lucy. I checked to see if he still had Megan on there, but he didn't. I sent her a message to see if she'd heard from him. She read it and didn't reply.

I was confused about all of it. I wanted to talk to Jake about it and see what he thought, but he'd not got out from under his duvet all day and was refusing to speak to either Debbie or me unless it was to ask for food.

Right before I went to bed, I tried Nathan again – still no answer. I didn't have a clue what I should do the next day when I saw him at school. Ignore him, shout at him, or punch him in the face?

Just as I was falling asleep in Jake's bed, I got a text from Polly:

Ed went mental at me for fucking off, he was so vexed and wouldn't shut up till I told him where I was. Said we looked after Jake. He thinks we're shagging. Even though I've told him to go fuck himself, he's gunning for you, I'm really sorry – just thought I'd warn you. xxx

I locked my phone and threw it on the floor. I lay there for ages, wondering how one party could mess everything up. It was completely insane. I looked out the window and prayed so hard for a snow day, even though it was so clear I could see the moon. I was dreading going into school the next day like you wouldn't believe.

Nine

We were sitting in a circle in the therapy room. Josie was opposite, staring at me intensely. Like a maniac. I wanted to tell her to do one, to stop it. To look at someone else. She was getting on my nerves. Every time I looked up, she was still looking.

I gave her the filthiest look I could, and turned my attention back to the lady doing our group therapy that morning.

Group therapy was the only time of day you'd be a hundred per cent sure you were in the loony bin. Once they'd had their regular morning debate on whether or not today would be the day I'd start talking again, we had to state our goals for the day. That was my favourite bit. I sat there, totally silent, obviously, and listened to how outrageous the rest of them actually were.

Today's goals were, as follows:

Blake: To find the key to the stationery cupboard, because that was the doorway to the actual Narnia. Fact. (Despite Caitlin screaming in his face that it was all lies.)

Caitlin: To prove Blake wrong, find her pink hairband that she's sure Josie stole off her, and to try and get me to start talking.

Josie: Nothing. Fuck us all. We're all idiots. She hates the world.

We talked about what we'd had for breakfast and Caitlin grassed up Josie for giving hers to Blake when nobody was looking. Josie told Caitlin she was a little bitch, and Caitlin got up and went to smack Josie, but Josie caught Caitlin's arm and twisted it round her back. The screaming was mental. I think my ear drum might have burst. In the end, Caitlin was taken back to her room by one of the nurses and we were dismissed.

In the corridor, Josie grabbed my arm. 'Adam,' she said.

I pulled my arm out of her grip in a way that told her to get off and leave me alone. I was still angry with her for grassing me up. I was angry with myself, too. I shouldn't have trusted her.

'Sorry,' she said. 'I'm really sorry.' She pulled her jumper sleeve up to her mouth and started chewing on it.

I didn't care if she was sorry. I wanted to get back to my room. I wanted to carry on writing stuff down for David. Even though I'd written down what had happened at the Christmas party, I wasn't feeling too bad. I was relieved that writing it all down hadn't brought back any of the panic and nightmares. I had the numb feeling, but numb I could deal with. Numb wasn't sitting bolt upright at 3 a.m. after the worst nightmare in the world, sweating and wondering if I was going to throw up.

'Hate to break up the party,' Damian said. 'I need you.' He pointed at me and took me away from Josie. I could have kissed him; I was so grateful.

He sniffed my hair, lifted my arm up, and sniffed my armpit then stepped away. He screwed up his face but was sort of smiling at the same time.

'You might want to go down and freshen yourself up a bit,' he said.

If I had the capability to feel anything, I'm sure offended would have been at the top of the list.

'You've got a very pretty girl waiting in there for you,' he winked and used his head to gesture towards the door behind him which was the Visitors' Room. 'One I'm pretty certain you wouldn't want thinking that you've lost the ability to wash, if you know what I mean?'

Polly.

I ran and skidded down the corridor into my room, sprayed some deodorant, brushed my teeth and skidded back so fast, with my heart racing the whole time.

'And there was me thinking you were emotionally detached from the world,' Damian said as I got back to where he was waiting for me. 'She must be someone special, eh? Go on, then.' He smiled and patted me on the back as I opened the door.

Polly was sitting on one of the old sofas, coat still on, and hunched over defensively.

I stopped by the door. She looked up at me from under the hood of her parka. She didn't smile, she didn't wave, she didn't say hello. She just looked at me. We stayed like that, staring at each other, for what seemed like a lifetime until the door opened and Damian walked in.

'You're still being supervised,' he whispered in my ear.

My shoulders sunk down low, along with my heart. I knew Polly would get all defensive and stroppy if someone else was there with us. She wouldn't be able to say what she wanted to; but then, of all the nurses, I was glad it was Damian and not one of the others.

'Well, go and sit down then,' he said, almost pushing me towards her.

I wobbled across the room and sat on the sofa opposite her.

'You're really not talking?' She asked.

In between us was a table with tea and little packets of biscuits on. She had already poured herself a cup, but the cup meant for me was empty.

'So we do what, exactly, just sit here in silence and look at each other?'

I couldn't even begin to tell you how I felt seeing her, because I didn't know, all I knew was that I couldn't take my eyes off her. It was sort of like when you meet someone famous. They don't seem real and you're completely fascinated by them.

'Can I ask you a question?' She asked Damian, who had plonked himself on a chair in the corner and was reading a newspaper.

'Sure thing,' he said, putting his paper down and coming over.

'What can I do? I mean, I'm here, yeah, but I'm way out of my depth, I haven't got a clue what I'm supposed to do, or say, or what.'

'I think it might be enough for Adam just to know that you

101

cared enough to come,' Damian said. He rubbed Polly's shoulder and left us to it.

'I don't know why I'm here,' she said. She picked up a pack of bourbons off the table and opened them aggressively. 'I mean, my mum and dad went mental the day you ended up in hospital. They said that enough was enough, and that what happened to Jake had nothing to do with me, and it wasn't my responsibility to make you better or anything.' She dunked the bourbon in her mug of tea and put it in her mouth, sucking on it before shoving it in.

'I wasn't even there that night, Adam. I wasn't even there. I was in the bloody Lake District with my stupid bloody family,' she said with her mouth full.

I sat back and crossed my arms. I let her carry on saying what she needed to say. It wasn't like I could contribute, or argue, or anything. Out of the corner of my eye, I could see that Damian was only pretending to read his paper; he hadn't turned the page in ages, which meant he was listening to her.

'Your doctor told me that you've been writing down what happened?'

I nodded.

'Have you got any paper?' She asked Damian. 'And a pen?' She turned to me. 'We can talk that way,' she said.

Damian looked concerned. 'I can't leave Adam to go and get you any, I'm afraid,' he said.

Polly sat back and did a really aggravated sigh. 'I don't know what I'm meant to do. I have no idea. This is just too much to take in, too much, Ads.' She leant forwards, and put her face in her hands, and I knew she was crying.

I wanted to get up and put my arm around her, to let her cry on my shoulder, but I couldn't. It worked in the same way that not talking did. I wanted to do it, to go to her, but there was some sort of invisible force stopping me. The intention was there, but something had happened in the wiring of my brain which meant the intention and the action just wouldn't marry up.

When she stopped crying and looked up, I couldn't decide if she was angry or scared. 'Have you got any idea what it was

102

like to find you that day?' She asked. 'On the landing?' She took a deep breath. 'I thought you were dead,' she said, and then the crying got worse. Damian came over with a box of tissues and sat next to her. I watched him comfort her. He rubbed her back and helped her to sip her tea.

What I felt, I'm sure, was guilt. I closed my eyes so I couldn't see her, but I opened them again quickly because I didn't want to not see.

I'm sorry. That was all I wanted to say. Three words. Three syllables. So much meaning.

It wouldn't come out.

When she'd calmed down, she sat up straight and took something out of her pocket. It was a small, white envelope with my name on it.

'I knew this would happen. I knew I'd get all emotional and not be able to handle it, so I wrote it all down instead,' she said. She put the envelope on the table. 'I don't want you to read it now. Read it later when I'm gone.'

She got up and zipped up her parka.

I wanted to get up and hug her and not let go, but my body wouldn't move.

Damian's face was full of pity, but I wasn't sure if it was for me, or for her, or maybe for us both.

'I'll see you soon,' she said, and her voice was shaking with tears again.

She left the room without looking back. I swallowed hard because I had that pain you get in the back of your throat when you're about to start crying. That threw me, that sudden feeling of emotion. It was alien to me. I'd stopped being able to feel anything weeks ago.

Damian sat down opposite me. 'It was a thought that had occurred to me, too, about trying to get you to communicate by writing things down, but David said no,' he said. 'He said he wanted to focus on you telling him what happened first.'

I nodded. I was glad because I thought that if I had to start talking to people, even if it was by writing stuff down, it would confuse my brain even more. The less I had to think about, the better.

Damian picked up the envelope Polly had left on the table. 'I'm going to have to let David read this first,' he said. 'In the meantime, why don't you go and chill out with the others in the rec room? I'll get him to bring it along to you later.' We stood up and walked towards the door.

I didn't want to hang out with the others. I wanted to go back to my room and sleep and think about Polly but because I was under supervision still, and Damian was the one supervising, I didn't have a choice.

I was sitting in the corner of the rec room watching Caitlin and Blake have a full-blown argument about who got to be which colour counter in Connect Four.

David caught my eye and in his hand was Polly's letter. We walked back to my room. I sat on my bed and he pulled up a chair.

'I think you should read it,' he said holding out the letter. 'But I'm going to sit here while you do, is that OK?'

I nodded and took it from him. It had been all I could think about all afternoon, and I'd gone through so many different theories in my head as to what it said. Maybe she didn't want to know me anymore, and the letter was a goodbye. That was the theory I'd pretty much decided was true, so my hands were shaking as I crossed my legs up on the bed and pulled the paper out of the envelope.

I looked up at David.

He nodded in approval.

Dear Adam,

I don't even know where to start, if I'm honest.

It's hard for all of us, what happened to Jake. We never think it's going to happen to us, do we?

See Adam, I can't walk away from this even if I wanted to. I know we're only sixteen and seventeen but I know I love you. I've never told you this before, but I always had a crush on you before you came to our party that night. I'd just never had the guts to tell you before. I know what everyone thinks about me, that I'm this hard and scary girl but deep down I'm not, deep down everything hurts. My parents hurt me, Ed hurts me, what happened to Jake hurt me, and seeing you the way you are because of it, and knowing that there's nothing I can do to make it better for you, that hurts me, too.

Your doctor told me about you writing down everything that happened. I offered to tell him what happened after the party, but he said he wants to hear your version first which I think is good.

I want you to get better. I've been doing a lot of stuff outside to try and help. I've spoken to my mum and dad and told them that I'm going to be there for you, and I don't care what they think. There's nothing they can do about it, I'm sixteen and can make my own decisions. Ed was on their side. He wanted me to walk away from it all, but the other night we got a bit drunk together and we had a heart to heart and he's changed his mind. He said he might even come in and see you himself. He wondered if it might help. A total 180, but I think before he was just scared. I think we all are.

I went to see Debbie, too, but she wasn't in. I wrote her a letter and put it through the door. I know how much you need her, Adam. I don't know if I've done the right thing but I'm hoping she'll find it in her heart to forgive you and come and see you.

There's only one more thing I want to say and I don't care if you hate me for it. Imagine if Jake could see you like this, Adam. What would he say? If he knew you'd given up so easily? How gutted would he be? You need to try your hardest to get better, Adam. I know that you're scared, but try really hard.

This is not easy for me, but I'm not giving up on you so I'll be in to see you again soon.

Polly xxx

I put the letter back in the envelope and put it under my pillow. It was too much to take in at once. I knew I'd want to read it again later. I pushed away the thoughts of what Jake would say. I didn't want to think about it now.

'You OK?' David asked.

I shrugged.

'Do you think you can carry on telling me what happened after the Christmas party?' He asked.

I nodded. I genuinely felt, for the first time since I'd got there, that I could. Polly's letter had given me hope. Seeing her had made me feel something and, even though I wasn't sure what it was I felt, I knew it was a big step.

I nodded at David again, just to make sure he'd seen.

'You're doing well, Adam,' he said. He smiled at me as he left the room, and I carried on where I left off.

'Where's Jake?' Nathan slapped me on the back as I walked through the school gates the Monday morning after the drama of the weekend. He was smiling and acting like nothing had happened.

I gave him a filthy look.

'What?'

I gave him another filthy look.

'Be a dickhead, then,' he said.

I sighed. 'Debbie let him have the day off. He's upset about Kelly.'

'Yeah, about that ...'

I thought about saying nothing and just walking away: it would have been easier. I didn't want to have to deal with it. I just wanted it to be OK, for us all to be friends again. As we carried on walking up the path, I could feel the tension between us so I had to say something to him about it. If I didn't, it'd just get worse.

'Why did you go off with him, Nath? I couldn't believe you just got into the car and left like that. Didn't you see the state of Jake? And Megan. You're–'

'Oi seriously, leave it–'

'No. I'm not leaving it, you proper turned weird and took the piss, you've been nowhere to be seen all weekend, ignoring me and I can't–'

'Hang on a sec,' Nathan said. He stopped walking and grabbed my arm for me to stop, too. 'Megan dumped me on Saturday night. Where were you for me?'

'What? But–'

'Exactly.' He smiled smugly, pulled his bag up on his shoulder, and carried on walking.

'Nath?' I followed him. 'You'd just had a row with her, that's all, and I tried to ask you, but Danny said you didn't want to talk about it, remember?'

He carried on walking, ignoring me.

'She was outside with Jake, he'd talked her into leaving you to calm down, then going in and sorting it all out, until we saw you holding hands with the exact girl who'd caused the row in the first place. This is all bullshit. You've been ignoring us all *weekend ... I–'*

'You think it's easy for me?'

'What?'

'You two?'

'Who two?'

'You and Jake?'

'Me and Jake? What are you talking about?'

'You two have always been well close.'

'We're all close.'

'Yeah, OK,' his voice was full of sarcasm. 'You two have known each other forever. I've only been knocking around–'

'We've been best friends, all of us, for five years, Nathan.'

'Yeah, and you and Jake have been best friends since you were three.'

'You're saying you went off with Danny because you think me and Jake are closer?'

'I'm saying maybe I'm getting a little bit fucked off with how close you two are. How much of a spare part I am. Piggy in the middle, y'know? Where were you two for me on Saturday? Jake was outside with Megan, of all people, and you ... you were trying to get laid with Ed's little sister. I got mugged off by you both, so I figured it was time I found myself some new friends.'

I couldn't believe what I was hearing. 'You're not serious, are you? Jake was outside, calming Megan down and getting her to come in and make up with you,' I said.

'And where were you? When I told you to sit down for a drink, all you were worried about was finding Jake.' He raised his eyebrows at me.

'Nath, I just didn't wanna sit with–'

'Neither of you were there for me,' he interrupted. 'You know who was there for me Saturday? Danny. He was a friend to me when I needed someone. He saw me on my own, he invited me to join him and his mates, he cheered me up. Just what you and Jake should have been doing.'

'So we make one mistake and you dump us for Danny?'

'And what?'

'He's bad news.'

'Shut up, Ad. Leave it now, yeah?' He shook his head at me,

109

pulled his bag up on his shoulder and walked off, leaving me feeling like I was spinning on the spot.

At lunch, I was looking for Megan to see what was going on when Ed appeared in front of me. Out of nowhere. Like a bloody ninja. I was caught off guard.

'A quiet word?' He asked, with his head cocked to the side and his eyebrows raised.

He spun around to walk next to me, put his arm around me and guided me gently round the back of the science block. I was shitting myself.

'She said she'd text you to tell you where she was,' I said, panicked.

'I know, she told me. She flipped out at me this morning over a bowl of Rice Krispies,' Ed said. 'She also told me that you didn't try it on at all.' He moved so he was standing right in front of me, staring me straight in the eyes. 'Was she telling the truth?'

'Yes, she was telling the truth,' I said.

'Do you like her?'

I sighed and looked away.

'That's a yes,' he said. 'Look, you're alright, Adam. All I'm saying is that if you hurt her, I'm going to shit on your head, do you understand?'

'Yep, can I go now?'

'We're OK,' Ed said, moving out of the way. 'You understand why I needed to talk to you, yes?'

'She's your sister, I get it,' I said.

'She's a pain in my fucking arse, Adam, and she'll be a pain in yours, but I'm telling you, I do love the guts off her, and if you hurt her–'

'You'll shit on my head,' I said.

He smiled.

'You sorted things out with Nath yet? I heard he bunked off with Danny on Saturday, man, that was harsh,' he said.

'I know right,' I said as we both walked back round to the main path together. 'He's saying me and Jake are out of order 'cause we weren't there for him when Megan dumped him, but I *didn't even have a chance. He told me to go off to find Jake and come back. Next thing I know, him and Danny are best mates and he's doing one off into the night with him.'*

'Look, don't worry about it, Danny will get bored of him before long, he always does. He doesn't keep friends the way the rest of us do. He picks them up and puts them back down again when he wants to. This won't last long,' he said.

'Really?' I asked.

'Really,' he said. 'He's a twat, always has been ever since we were little.'

'Cool, thanks,' I said.

'No worries, bro.' He saluted me as he walked off to catch up with his mates.

'Where's Nath?' Jake asked from inside his sofa cocoon. Tom and Jerry *was on in the background. The whole thing reminded me of the time he had the flu when he was ten, and spent a whole week cuddled up on the sofa under his duvet, watching TV while I was at school.*

'Dunno,' I said and sat on the other sofa. 'How you feeling? Heard anymore from Kel?'

'What do you mean, you don't know?' He sat up and looked at me. 'Why's he not come back? Was he not in school?'

I reached for the TV guide to try and distract myself. I was going to have to tell him what Nathan had said, but I didn't really want to. He was heartbroken enough about Kelly, without having to deal with Nathan dumping us for Danny over something so stupid, it didn't even really matter. All that stuff about Jake and I being close and him being left out was rubbish. I didn't want to dump it all on Jake while he was feeling like this.

'What's going on?' Jake said.

'He's just being a dick, that's all.'

'Because of that Danny? Yeah, I was thinking about it earlier and I reckon it's 'cause of that Sarah, too. He just fancies her and that's why he went off with her.' He reached out for the remote and paused the TV.

Nathan and Sarah were holding hands as they left. I wished

111

Nathan hadn't said what he'd said earlier. I much preferred Jake's theory.

I shrugged.

'Nah, nah, nah, you know more,' he said. 'What's he said?'

I cleared my throat.

'Just tell me, was it about Kelly?'

I sighed and put the TV guide down. 'I'm gonna go and get a Coke, want one?' I stood up.

'Get one in a minute, tell me what he said.'

'He didn't say anything.'

'You're such a liar,' Jake said and un-paused the TV.

Debbie was in the kitchen emptying the washing machine. She was knelt down next to it, huffing, sighing, and pulling all the clothes out. The radio was playing some sort of talk show thing.

I opened the fridge.

'Christ, you frightened the life out of me,' she said.

'Any Coke in here, Deb?' I asked.

'In the salad drawer, darling.'

I got one out and shut the fridge. She stood with her hands on her hips, staring at me.

'What's up? I know that tone of voice anywhere. What's wrong?' she asked.

I took a deep breath.

'Your dad upset you again?' She shook her head in disgust at him, but for once it wasn't him.

'Nope,' I said.

She pulled out a chair for me at the kitchen table and one for herself. 'Sit,' she said.

'Do I have to?'

She nodded. 'Talk,' she said.

I opened my Coke and took a deep breath. 'You know Nathan went off with that Danny the other night?'

'I do. Jake has told me all of the details, he thinks it's because of that girl Sarah. Maybe he wanted to get back at Megan ... make her jealous–'

'It's not because of Sarah,' I said.

She got up to put the kettle on. We all knew it was a serious

112

chat with Debbie when the kettle went on for her coffee. 'No?'

I shook my head. 'Nathan was angry because me and Jake weren't there for him when it kicked off with him and Megan. He told me earlier that he thinks me and Jake are close and leave him out and that he wants to find new friends. Like Danny.'

'Oh,' she said, leaning on the side.

I watched her, waiting for her to say more. She'd have the right words to make it better. She always did. 'And this Danny, Jake said he's bad news?'

I shrugged. 'Apparently.'

Debbie sighed. 'Thing is, darling, there's not a lot you can do, is there?'

'What do you mean?'

'Nathan's perfectly entitled to go off and make new friends.'

'But–'

'But it sucks, and it hurts and you want everything to stay the same, just how it is … forever. But it won't. Things change. People change.'

'I don't like it,' I said.

'I know you don't. You can still be friends with Nathan, just maybe not as close.'

I was completely thrown by her comment. I didn't agree. We had each other. We didn't need anyone else.

'I know it's scary, sweetheart,' she said. 'Especially for you, you've lost so much already, but you just have to remember that Nathan having new friends doesn't mean he's not your friend anymore.' She stopped talking and got her mug out of the dishwasher.

'I don't like Danny,' I said.

'I know, but my advice would be to let Nathan do what he's got to do.'

'But it's upset me, Deb.'

She stopped, walked over to me and put her hand on my head. 'Of course it has, darling, all change is scary.'

'But Danny's an arsehole. What if Nathan gets in trouble because of him?'

'Nathan knows better than that,' she said.

She pulled away and went back to making her coffee. 'So, talk to me about Polly ...' she said.

'Nothing to tell,' I said, shrugging.

She smirked at me as I got up and walked out of the room, trying to hide my smile.

After three hours of the silent treatment from Jake, because I wouldn't say what had happened with Nathan and why he didn't come back after school, I finally told him. Step by step, blow by blow. Then I told him what Debbie had said about it all, too.

He was sitting on the wall outside the chippy, deep in thought. He held a chip mid-air, stopped on its way to his mouth. It was like someone had paused him. I stood in front of him, waiting for him to speak.

'I have no words,' he said, and put the chip in his mouth.

I sat down next to him on the wall and opened my drink. He took it off me and had a long swig.

'Even if he is pissed off with us for not being there for him, or whatever, it's not right is it?' He held another chip in front of his mouth. 'Actually, he's probably got the right to be a bit pissed off with me, 'cause I didn't go and find him as soon as I found out what happened.'

'It's not your fault, you were trying to calm Megan down and get her to sort it out with him,' I said.

'He'll get over it,' he said. 'All this bullshit about us being closer and yada yada ... ignore him. He's being an idiot.' He got up off the wall and took his vinegar-soaked battered sausage out of the packet. 'Now tell me what the deal is with you and Polly?' He took a huge bite of his sausage.

'Don't you want to talk about what happened with Kelly?' I asked him. I didn't want to talk to him about Polly. It still didn't seem right to be getting all excited about it while he was totally heartbroken.

'Nope, I do not want to talk about that slut,' he said. 'Unless you saw her at school today and she was ... No, I don't want to talk about her.'

'There's nothing to tell about Polly,' I said.

'Did you see Kelly today?' He asked.

I laughed to myself. 'No, I didn't actually.'

'Cool,' he said.

'So, you gonna go out with Polly then?' He asked.

I was just about to answer when a car skidded to a halt next to us. Its bass was throbbing. The tinted window on the passenger side rolled down and a cloud of smoke escaped, followed by Nathan's head.

'Alright gay boys?' He laughed.

Jake and I watched him as he got out, shut the door, and then leant his hand in to grab a fiver off the driver.

'Whatcha up to then?' He asked.

'Eating our chips,' Jake said. His tone was half-dead. 'You?'

'Getting some dinner for me and Danny boy, then we're off round Sarah's, innit.' He smiled and winked.

'Oi, hurry up, man.' Danny's voice came from inside the car.

I looked at Jake, then at Nathan, then back at Jake, then back at Nathan. Then I spoke.

'Nath, man, what you doing?'

'Getting chips.'

He smiled, smacked me on the back, and went inside the chippy.

'Did that just happen?' I asked Jake as we walked off.

'I don't know,' he said, glancing over his shoulder. 'I think it might have.'

'That was weird,' I said.

As we turned the corner, Danny's car skidded behind us, he revved up the engine, and as it screeched past, the sound of Nathan's voice came flying towards us. 'Loooooooooosers,' it said.

I threw my chips in the next bin. I'd suddenly lost my appetite.

Nathan had spent a few days ignoring us outside school, but in school he was pretending nothing had happened. It was completely doing my head in. We were only good enough for

115

him when Danny wasn't around.

Three days before we broke up for Christmas, we were in the home-ec room about to bake mince pies for the carol concert that night.

We were asked get into pairs.

Nathan made a beeline for Jake, grabbed him, moved him over to a kitchen unit and left me standing there on my own.

'Loner,' he said.

'Adam, you'll have to work on your own. Do you think you can handle it?' Our teacher asked when she saw there were no other people to pair up with. 'I'll put you here. You can still talk to them.' She moved me to the kitchen unit opposite Nathan and Jake.

At the unit in the corner, Kelly was trying to keep her head down. Jake kept glancing over at her.

'You OK?' I asked him.

'He's fine, aren't you Jakey boy?' Nathan said, patting him on the back before he'd even had the chance to respond to me.

'I haven't got a clue what I'm doing,' I said, looking at all the ingredients.

'You gotta read the recipe, idiot,' Nathan said.

Jake glanced at Kelly again. It was the closest he'd come to her since the party. She wasn't usually in any of our classes but because today was a special thing, we'd all been mixed up.

'Look, Jake, just don't worry about it,' Nathan said. 'The first thing you got to do is block her on Facebook and delete her number. Forget about her. She's a skank.' He punched Jake lightly on the arm, then opened the packet of flour and started weighing it out.

'I can't believe she did that to me, man,' Jake said.

'I know, she's a dirty cheating ho,' Nathan said.

'I feel like my heart's been ripped out, you know,' he said to Nathan.

'You know what? You need someone to take your mind off her,' Nathan said. 'When I was with Megan, I thought nobody would ever be as good as her ...' He poured the flour into their bowl. 'Then I met Sarah ...' He gazed off out the window. 'She's amazing. Trust me, you need someone new, someone better.'

116

Jake shook his head. 'How's Polly?' He asked me. Probably because he wanted to change the subject.

'Polly?' Nathan asked. 'Is something going on with you two?' He laughed so loudly that most of the class looked over.

Jake thumped him on the arm. 'Stop being an idiot, Nath, or I swear to God I'm going to throw that whole packet of flour over your head.'

'Why did nobody tell me about this?' Nathan asked.

'Er, because you've not been around,' I said.

'Er, because you're an idiot, actually,' he said. He laughed away to himself for a bit, then looked up at me. 'You do know Ed's gonna rip your bollocks off, don't you?'

'No, he's not,' I said.

'Yeah, he will,' Nathan waved a spoon in my face. 'Then you won't be able to do anything with her. Not that you know what to do anyway, Mr Virgin the Virginal.'

I didn't want to rise to it so I ignored him.

'Ed and Ads already spoke about it and he's cool,' Jake said. 'So shove that up your a-hole, and get mixing this pastry, bitch.'

'Serious?' Nathan asked, as he shoved his hands into their bowl of mixture. I was still weighing out mine.

'Yep,' was all I said.

'What's the matter with you, Billy no-mates?' Nathan asked.

'Nothing,' I said.

'You're lagging,' Nathan said, as I opened the butter. 'Anyway, back to more important issues,' he said.

'Like?' Jake asked.

'Like finding you something to help you get over that slut in the corner.'

Jake gave him a sideways look. 'Unless it's a supermodel, or vouchers for a year's supply of Nando's, I doubt it,' he said.

'I had something more specific in mind,' Nathan said, grinning.

I put my flour down and leant in. I had a feeling I didn't want to miss this one. 'Like?' I asked.

'Not that it's any of your business,' he said to me, then turned to Jake. 'You know that girl who was with us Saturday

117

night, not Sarah, her mate Lucy?'

'The ones you ditched us for?' I asked him.

He gave me a filthy look.

'Anyway,' Nathan said, making a point of turning his body away from me and towards Jake. 'She fancies you, man.'

I snorted and shook my head.

'I don't remember her,' Jake said. 'Show me her on Facebook.'

'Danny said you should come and hang out with us,' Nathan said, getting out his phone. 'He thinks you're cool.'

'How can he think Jake's cool?' I asked. 'He doesn't even know him.'

'Don't be jel, Ads, just because he doesn't think you're alright.' Nathan shook his head at me. He handed his phone to Jake.

Jake turned his nose up. 'Nah, she's not my type,' he said, and went back to what he was doing.

'You should think about it,' Nathan said. 'Danny's OK, you know.'

'Nah, it's OK,' Jake said. His head darted around to the corner. Kelly looked up at him, then straight back down. Jake sighed.

I gave him my best sympathetic smile.

'Think about it,' Nathan said, putting his phone back in his pocket. 'It'll help, I promise.'

'Just because you didn't even stop to piss between girls, doesn't mean Jake's gonna be the same,' I said. I slammed my flour down on the worktop and some of it exploded out the top, into a puff of smoke in my face. I ignored them both laughing at me trying to bat the flour cloud away. If Jake had liked Lucy, and started hanging out with them all, I'd be on my own again. All because Danny didn't think I was cool.

'Shut up, Ads,' Nathan said.

'Why you being like this?' I asked him.

'Like what?'

'Don't act all innocent,' I said.

'Ads is right you know, Nath. You need to stop acting like the hard man just 'cause you got your new hard friend Danny,' *he tapped him affectionately on the shoulder. Nathan jolted his shoulder away.*

'See, this is what I mean about you two. You're always ganging up on me, and you wonder why I'm hanging about with Danny? At least he makes me feel like I belong,' he said. His eyes were watering like he was about to cry.

'Nath,' Jake whispered. 'It's OK, you do belong here with us. You're our friend.'

Nathan took a deep breath in, then sighed. 'Yeah, OK,' he said.

Jake ignored his sarcasm, smiled at him, took the mixed-up pastry out the bowl, slammed it onto the worktop, and handed Nathan the rolling pin.

I didn't know how Jake could stay so calm with him, when all I wanted to do was launch myself over the worktop, grab him, and wring his neck.

When we'd finished the mince pies, we were told we could go straight home if we wanted to, or we could hang around, and see if there was anything else we could help with.

'Come on then, boys,' Jake said. 'That is, if you're coming?' He asked Nathan.

'Yeah, I am as it goes.'

'I'm going to hang around and wait for Polly,' I said. She didn't know I was waiting. I hadn't planned it. It would be the first time ever that I'd not walked home with Jake, and gone back to his for dinner, but I just wanted to get away from Nathan.

Jake's jaw hit the floor. 'You're not coming back to mine?'

'Nah, I'm gonna—'

'Ah, see that,' Nathan jabbed me in the ribs. 'You are a hypocrite. You can't go round saying I'm out of order for ditching you for Danny, when you're doing the exact same thing right now.'

'You know what, Nath, maybe I just don't want to be around you? Have you thought about that?'

'Why not? I'm awesome,' he said, smiling.

'I just want to see Polly, OK?'

'Suit yourself,' he said.

'Go, I'll catch you up, go shop and get me a chocolate bar.' Jake handed Nathan a pound.

'What?' I asked Jake. He was staring me in the face.

'He's well upset you, hasn't he?'

'What made you think that?'

'Don't be sarky, Ads,' he said. 'Look, ignore him. He's getting too big for his boots because of Danny, and Sarah and that, but it won't last. Remember what Ed said to you? We gotta be here for him when Danny turns him over,' he said.

I sighed.

'Your girl's coming.'

I followed his eye line to behind me where Polly was walking up to us, snuggled under the hood of her jacket and a really huge scarf. When she saw me, she smiled really widely.

'Have fun. Don't do anything I wouldn't.' Jake winked and walked off to catch up with Nathan.

Ten

I had the nightmare again.

In it, we're in the park. I'm sitting on the bench eating chips, and Jake and Nathan are playing football. I'm laughing at Jake and taking the piss out of him for missing a kick. It's amazing, just like old times, but then, out of nowhere, a massive gang of people comes over and a fight breaks out, and everyone starts beating Jake up.

I try to get off the bench, but I'm stuck, and I have to fight against this invisible force that's stopping me from moving. It's like trying to move in deep water. I can't. I can't get to him, and I struggle while I watch them take it in turns to stab him. Then they all run off and leave him to fall to the floor. He's lying there; the rain is beating down on his body and mixing with the blood and the mud.

Then the ground opens up beneath him and he falls into it. He just falls. He's gone. Into a hole in the ground and I can't move. I can't move to stop any of this happening, or to go and find him. He's gone.

When I woke up, I was screaming Jake's name over and over again. I sat up sweating, my heart racing, and I felt like I was about to throw up.

It was the first time I'd had it since I'd been there. That definitely wasn't a good thing.

There was a massive crash of thunder outside my window. The nurse watching came over to me with a cup of water.

'Are you OK, Adam?' She asked.

I ignored her. I got out of bed and walked out into the corridor. She followed me closely but didn't say anything. It was dark in the corridor; there was only a small light on at the nurses' station.

Another flash of lightning followed straight away by a crash of thunder.

In the dark rec room, I could make out Josie. She was looking out of the window with a blanket draped over her shoulders and was watching the storm. I went to turn around and walk back to my room, but it was too late, she'd seen me.

'Couldn't sleep either?' She asked.

I shook my head.

'I love a thunderstorm,' she said after another big flash and crash. She was looking out the window at the dark sky. 'Want to watch with me?'

I didn't move. I didn't want to watch it with her because I was still cross with her for grassing me up to the nurses and David.

She opened up her blanket. 'It's OK,' she whispered.

I was worried that if I went back to bed, the nightmare might happen again. Staying out there with her would be a good distraction. I went and sat next to her but I didn't let her wrap the blanket around me and she didn't try to force it.

As we sat there and watched the sky light up and then erupt with thunder, over and over again, I wished so much she was Polly. Then I felt bad for thinking that. Even though she grassed me up and betrayed my trust, deep down I knew it was only because she cared.

We sat there for ages. She said nothing to me, demanded nothing from me. We just watched the storm come and go until my nurse told us to get back to our rooms.

Josie let me take the blanket with me. It was warm and soft and it made me feel safe.

After breakfast and group therapy, Josie and I went back to the rec room with cups of tea and sat together with the blanket over our laps.

'We need an open fire and a 50-inch flat screen and all the movies we want to watch, don't we?' She said.

The TV was playing up, and two of the other patients were playing on the pool table. I didn't want to go back to my room after my nightmare the night before. I was feeling pretty restless and I could feel that Josie was, too.

'Can we go out for a fag, please?' She asked Damian, who was trying to get the TV to work.

He looked at her from where he was perched on the end of one of the sofas. 'Have you seen it out there?' He asked.

'We can take a brolly?'

'Nope, not while it's coming down in sheets, Jose,' he said. 'This things buggered.' He stood up and turned the TV off.

'You do realise you're going to have trouble on your hands, don't you?' Josie said.

''Cause of the TV?'

'Nope,' she sighed. 'Because of all the nicotine-deprived mental patients.'

'Bring it on,' he said with a wink. 'Nothing I can't handle.' He did a ninja move. Josie laughed and I smiled.

'Blimey, Adam, was that a smile?' Damian asked. 'That's progress, my man,' he winked. 'And if this lot turn on me today, I want you on my side, OK?'

I nodded.

'Right then, you two, if you're that bored why don't you go and join in music therapy?'

We both stared at him.

'It's dangerous in there,' Josie said. 'Didn't you hear about Caitlin beating Blake up with a drumstick?'

Damian shrugged. 'You can go and grab some paper and pens off the guys doing art? Just no scissors ...'

'Nah, we're OK,' Josie said, curling up her nose.

'Suit yourselves, just no moaning about being bored. There's plenty to do.'

I snuggled further under the blanket. I wondered if the smile did mean I was making good progress. I wondered if next time I wanted to speak and tried to, it would happen.

Maybe Damian was right, maybe I was getting better. I had been feeling it, but then the nightmare last night had thrown me off.

We got new cups of tea and some little packets of biscuits. Josie read a book and I sort of read over her shoulder, but also

123

watched the sky as the rain stopped, the clouds moved away and the sun started shining again. It was the longest I'd stayed out of my room since I'd been there. It was the first time I'd actually chosen to stay with Josie, rather than run away from her at lightning speed.

'Hate to break up what looks like the world's most amazing snuggle, you two,' Damian said. 'But you've got a visitor.'

'Good luck,' Josie said. She was looking over to the nurses' station. Confused, I turned around to see my dad standing there. He looked over and gave me an uncomfortable wave.

I walked over slowly.

'You alright, son?' He asked.

I didn't look at him.

'Right then,' David said, coming over. 'Go and get your shoes on, then and meet us back here,' he said. 'We're going to go for a nice walk.'

With every step I took towards my room, I hoped that some freak accident would take me out, so I didn't even have to spend a second with him.

Even though the sun had come out, it was windy and damp. It was the first time I'd gone outside since the day I'd had the fake cigarette with Josie. It felt strange to be walking and my legs felt a bit shaky, like they'd forgotten how to move further than twenty paces.

'So how you feeling, son?' Dad asked.

David was walking next to me and watching my face. He knew I wasn't talking still, but he was leaving me to answer if I wanted to, or could.

We walked in silence until we approached a picnic-type bench under a huge bamboo canopy in the middle of quite a nice garden.

'Shall we sit?' David asked.

I sat opposite both of them and regretted it straightaway. I felt like I was on trial, being questioned. A flash of the night I was in the police station in the interview room came into my head.

I distracted myself by eating the apple I'd brought with me

that was left over from breakfast.

'How's he been then, Doc?' Dad asked.

'You're stable, aren't you, Adam?' He turned to my dad.

I wondered why David hadn't mentioned the plan and being on suicide watch. Or maybe he already had, maybe that was why Dad had come. Maybe they'd decided not to mention it to me to try and keep things normal. I took a big bite of my apple. I was hoping they'd get bored quickly, and Dad would go, and I could go back upstairs and away from him.

'I'd like to gain a bit more insight into your life at home. Is it OK if I ask a few questions?' David was looking at my dad, who looked nervous.

'Is it just you and Adam at home?' He asked.

Dad nodded, but it was a cagey nod. It wouldn't have surprised me if he'd taken my being locked up in here as an opportunity to move Jackie in.

'And you work?'

Dad hesitated. Then spoke. 'I lost my job a few years back, after Jenny, Adam's mum, passed away.'

That was rubbish. He hadn't worked for years before that. Mum always worked. Dad had always been on the dole, wasting his money down the bookies. He got loads of money off the government for me when Mum died, but I only saw a score from that each week, and I had to use that to feed myself.

'OK. And you live in local-authority housing. Is that stable accommodation?'

Dad looked a bit pissed off, like he thought David was prying too much again.

'Yes, Jenny and I were young when Adam was born, we lived there since he was a baby. It's not been easy ...'

'That's OK,' David said. 'I'm just trying to grasp what levels of support Adam might need when he's eventually ready to leave us.'

I doubted that was true after what he'd said the other day about not letting me out till he knew I didn't want to kill myself anymore. I think he wanted to know about my childhood, my relationships with my parents. All shrinks do. They want to know at which point our parents messed us up.

125

Dad turned to me. 'Adam, I don't know how you feel about this, but I was going to ask Jackie to move in with us.'

Even though I could have predicted it, it still felt like I'd been punched in the stomach and winded. My jaw clenched and my lips tightened. David was watching me really closely.

'I think we could use a woman around, you know?' Dad said.

I reckoned she'd already got her feet under the table. She'd been itching to for years.

'Who is Jackie?' David asked. He knew who Jackie was, he'd read it in my pad. I looked at him, confused. He checked Dad wasn't looking, and gave me a nod, and a little wink.

'Jackie is my girlfriend,' Dad said. He was gazing at me. I stared him out. A proper stand-off.

'How long have you been in a relationship with Jackie?' David asked.

'Quite a while, years,' Dad said.

'Adam?' David was waiting for a reaction. He knew how I felt about her.

My legs were bobbing up and down furiously. The anger was there, in my body, shooting around through my veins at a million miles an hour, looking for an exit to explode out of.

No way did I want her there. It was bad enough that I had to go back there at all, let alone to her pretending to be wifey and mummy, but there was nothing I could do about it. It wasn't my house, it wasn't my decision.

I swung my legs around and stood up. I stormed off across the grounds, with David probably pissing his pants with worry that I was going to escape through a bush and out into the big wide world.

He chased after me, Dad after him.

I got back to the doors to our wing. They were locked. There was a buzzer on the door next to the key code thing. There were three wards listed on there, but I had no idea which one was mine.

I pushed all three buttons as they came up behind me.

My dad was huffing and puffing and red in the face.

'Come on then, Adam, let's get back upstairs and calm

down,' David said.

As soon as the door was open, I took the stairs two at a time, leaving them behind again. At the main door for our ward, I got stuck, because of the other door-entry thing but luckily Josie was just walking past. She waved down the nurse at the station who buzzed me in.

'You OK?' Josie asked.

I ignored her. I didn't want her talking to me. I didn't want anyone speaking to me, touching me, trying to make me laugh or telling me to play pool. I wanted everyone to leave me alone.

So my dad's only reason for coming in to see me was to tell me about Jackie. He wasn't there to offer me any support. He was meant to be there for me and love me but he had only come to get my approval to move that slapper into my mum's bed.

'Adam?' Josie called after me.

I kept walking, head down, straight into my room.

I sat down on my bed and rocked. The anger was still there, still flying through my veins, and I was trying to control it but I was raging at the thought of how selfish he was.

I hate him.

'Adam,' David poked his head round the door. 'How are you feeling?'

I didn't look at him.

'Would you like something to help calm you down?'

'Is he OK?' I heard Josie's voice.

'Not now, Josie. Go back to the rec area, please, this doesn't involve you.'

I sat on my bed, breathing deeply. I looked down at the floor because if I looked up, Dad might still have been there and, if I saw him, I would have launched myself at him, and hit him, or something.

'Adam, I think your dad wants to say something. Can he come in?' David was still there, watching me sway back and forth.

'Adam,' Dad's voice came out from the doorway. I looked at the floor and put my fingers in my ears. 'I'm sorry. I just don't know how to handle any of this. I don't know what it is you need or want from me, and you're not talking. If you were talking–'

I got up and pushed past him. I stormed across the corridor and went in to the shower room. I couldn't believe he'd just turned it round on me. If I was talking, he could what? Ignore everything I say anyway, because that's all he ever did.

There was a knock on the door.

'I'm going to go now,' Dad said.

Good. I didn't want to see him ever again.

He had never been a dad to me, so there was no point in pretending now.

Any hope I'd had after seeing Polly the day before had gone, along with any thought that I might have been getting better. I was back to where I started. Even the comfort of my emotions being numbed had disappeared and all I felt was anger. Anger at everyone for forcing me to try and get better when all I wanted was to die.

I had to get out of there. As soon as I was certain Dad had gone, I went back into my bedroom and picked up my pad and started writing so quickly and so furiously, it made my hand ache.

I let go of Polly's hand and opened my front door. I walked in first. The place was empty and quiet; Dad was out, thank God. I knew he'd embarrass me, maybe enough for Polly to change her mind, regret holding my hand all the way home and run all the way back to hers, screaming her head off.

'Smells funny in here,' she turned up her nose.

Oh God.

'Stale booze and fags?' I asked, and she nodded.

I hadn't been home for ages and the place was a tip. Even if housework had been a skill of my dad's, he was never here to do any.

'I'd offer you tea, but there won't be any milk,' I said. I grabbed a can of air freshener and took Polly straight up to my room.

'Don't worry,' she smiled.

I leant across her and opened my bedroom door and, as soon as she was in, I opened the curtains and the window and sprayed some of the air freshener about.

'Better?' I asked.

She stood in the space between the door and my bed and looked around. There wasn't much to see, just my furniture, a few books, my ancient TV ...

'Do you play?' She asked, picking up my guitar.

'A bit,' I said. 'There's a string broken, so not really anymore.'

'Why don't you get a new one?' She asked.

I shrugged. She wiped the dust off the guitar with the sleeve of her jacket, and started randomly strumming.

'Do you play?'

She looked at me and laughed. 'Does it sound like it?'

She put the guitar back and looked around the room again.

I took off my coat, took hers, and put the TV on. I wished it smelt nicer, was more homely, or at least that I could have made her a cup of tea.

'Sorry,' I said, as I hung our coats up on the back of the door.

'For what?'

'The state of this place. It's not exactly welcoming, is it?'

'I'm here to see you, Ads, not judge your house.'

She picked up one of the photo frames from my bedside table and laughed right from her belly. 'Is this you and Jake?' she shrieked. 'How old were you both?'

I loved that picture. 'It was taken on Jake's tenth birthday.' I sat down next to her and leant over to see it. 'He was meant to have a big bowling party but it snowed really badly. We basically ended up in the garden having snowball fights.'

'And making epic snowmen,' she said, touching the picture. Between Jake and I was our snowman. He'd taken us almost all day to build and he was huge, taller than we were.

'We named him Bobski,' I said. I looked at the photo, at Jake and I wrapped up in our coats, hats, scarves, and gloves, with huge smiles on our faces. I couldn't help but smile.

'What happened to Bobski?' Polly asked.

'He melted,' I laughed.

'So sad,' she said, pretending to wipe away a tear. 'I hope he's happy in snowman heaven.'

'After that picture was taken, Jake thought it'd be a really good idea to bobsleigh down the stairs in one of Debbie's washing baskets.'

'Noooooo, did he hurt himself?'

'Cracked his head open, blood everywhere.'

'What did you do?'

'I cried.'

She put her head on my shoulder, laughing. 'That's brilliant,' she said.

She put the photo back and picked up the one next to it. 'This is your mum, isn't it?' She asked.

I nodded.

'I know that because you look like her.' Her smile took away the sadness that was creeping up my throat. She held the picture up to the side of my head. 'Spitting image,' she said. Then she placed it back gently and perfectly.

Things were getting pretty intense. I was probably going to have to kiss her soon and I was really nervous about it. I'd never kissed anyone before. I stood up and pretended to wipe a bit of dust off my chest of drawers.

'How's Nathan being?' She shuffled back onto my bed a bit and crossed her legs.

'Bit of an idiot still,' I said. 'He was being a dick while we were making the mince pies today. He shoved me out and was trying to get Jake to agree to go out with that Sarah's mate.'

'Lucy?'

'Yeah.'

'That's crap. Danny'll get bored of him soon. Then he'll be back with his tail between his legs. Trust me.'

'I hope so,' I said, and I really did. I sat on the floor and picked up my guitar.

'It'll be OK,' Polly said.

I shrugged. 'Thing is, I can see he might have been pissed off with us, but dumping us for Danny like that. And ... this thing with Lucy and Jake–'

'You're worried he's going to take Jake away, too?'

I nodded.

'That's never going to happen.'

I couldn't make sense of the new Nathan. All I could do was cling to the hope that both Ed and Polly were right, and Danny would get bored of him, and then everything could go back to how it was before.

Polly cleared her throat.

I looked up at her.

'Am I going to have to come down there or what?'

'Huh?'

She slid down onto the floor next to me, took my guitar, put it gently to the side, then wrestled me on to my back.

Then she was straddling me, pinning my hands down above my head, her face inches from mine.

'I have to warn you, I've never kissed anyone before; I might be shit at it,' she said.

I smiled. I smiled because her blatant honesty took all my nervousness away.

'Neither have I,' I whispered as she leant in closer.

'Good, then we'll have nothing to compare it to, as far as we know, we're the best kissers in the entire universe.'

She was still smiling as her lips touched mine.

131

'Whoa, look who looks like the cat who's got the cream?' Jake said as I strode towards them with a mouth full of chips.

Even though it was only the afternoon, it was almost dark already. The streetlights in the park had just flicked on. The cold was biting my neck. I was going to have to convince them both to go back to Jake's. I was freezing. It was OK for them in their big jackets and beanies.

'And we've not seen him for all of Thursday night, all day Friday and half of Saturday. Does that mean what we think it means?' Nathan asked.

I sat down on the bench next to them and completely ignored the fact they were both staring at me. I just carried on eating my chips. While grinning.

'Spill,' Jake said, taking my chips off me and giving them to Nathan.

'Oi, that's my breakfast, lunch, and dinner,' I said.

'And you can have it back when you give us the gory details,' Nathan asked.

'Nice to see you here at the weekend, and not off with your boyfriend Danny,' I stuck my middle finger up at him.

'Oooooooh, the sex has made him all cocky and shit,' he said.

'For your information, I have not had sex with her,' I said, taking my chips back from him.

'Liar,' he said.

Jake looked me square in the eyes, took my wrist, and felt for my pulse.

'What are you doing?' I asked.

'He's checking to see if you're still alive, you know, like an alive, breathing, human who actually wants to have sex, and not some sort of frigid corpse.'

'I'm not, actually,' Jake said. 'I'm checking to see if he's lying. I saw a programme about how people's pulses change, like go faster I think, when they're lying ... You're not lying, are you?'

'Nope,' I said.

'Then if you haven't been in bed with her for two whole days, where the hell have you been?'

132

'Well, Thursday night we went round to the shop, got some tea, milk, and biscuits, and sat talking—'

'Talking?' Nathan spat.

I ignored him and carried on. 'Yesterday we bailed on school, with it being the last day of term, and we went to that park. We were gonna get out one of those pedalo things but they don't do them in the winter, then it started raining; so we ended up huddled under that bandstand thing holding hot cups of tea I bought us from the tea hut—'

'How romantic,' Nathan laughed.

'Then when we got back, we chilled at hers, listening to music and stuff. This morning, I've been asleep.' I grabbed the last few chips out my box and shoved them in my mouth.

'And there was no shagging, at any point?' Jake asked.

'Nope.'

'Look into my eyes,' he grabbed my head and turned it round to his.

'Nope,' I said again.

'So you, like, dated her?' Nathan asked.

'I'm aware of the fact that being a gentleman might be a bit of an alien concept to you, Nathan, owing to your current attitude problem but, yes, that is exactly what I did.' I smirked at him.

'Fuck off,' he said, leaning back onto the bench and out of my view.

'Did you at least touch her tits?' Jake asked.

'Yeah,' I said.

'Anything else?'

I nodded.

'Good.' He patted me on the back. 'You be a gentleman then my friend. A part of a dying breed.' He nodded, jumped off the bench, and grabbed the football.

'Nice to see you've graced us with your presence for once,' I said to Nathan.

'You can talk,' he said. 'Anyway, I'm not sticking around for long,' he pointed over to the gate where Sarah and Lucy were walking into the park.

'Looky looky looky,' Nathan said standing up.

Jake looked at me with a screwed-up face. 'I hope she's not come to try and pull me,' he whispered as he sat down next to me. 'She'll be very disappointed. She's just not good enough for the Jake loving.'

I laughed and opened my can of Coke as we watched Sarah wrap her arms around Nathan. He picked her up off the floor and span her around.

'You two best go in the bushes if you're gonna get up to stuff,' Lucy said. 'Nobody wants to see that.' She walked away from them and over to us.

She stopped right in front of Jake, put her hand on her hips, cocked her head to the side, and smiled. 'You're as good-looking as I remember,' she said. She opened her mouth slightly and bit her tongue. I think she was trying to be seductive or something, but she looked like a bit of an idiot.

Last time a girl came on to Jake while we were sitting on this bench, Jake took the bait and ended up with her for five months. Somehow, I didn't see this going the same way, judging by the stony cold look on his face.

'You forgotten how to talk?' She asked.

'Nope,' Jake said.

'Oh, so you're just rude?'

'Nah, I'm just cold and I want Nathan to hurry the fuck up so we can go home,' he said.

'Yeah, it is cold, innit?' She said.

'Freezing,' I said.

'Who's your friend, Jake?' She asked.

'Adam,' he said.

'Oh, Adam,' she laughed. 'You're Adam,' she said, pointing at me. 'Yeah, Danny's told me about you.'

I didn't know what to say.

'Danny's told you about Adam?' Jake asked. 'What's he said?'

'That he's a proper loser,' Lucy held her stomach in an exaggerated laugh.

Jake went to stand up, but I put my arm in front of him. 'Leave it,' I whispered.

'What, you can't stand up for yourself?' Lucy looked at me

134

with her hands on her hips. *'Anyway,'* she turned to Jake. *'About you being good-looking.'*

Jake snorted and turned his head away.

'Did Nathan tell you what I said?'

'Yeah, he did,' Jake said.

'You fancy going out, then?' She asked him.

'Nah, it's OK,' Jake said, standing up.

Nathan and Sarah came over, holding hands.

'Your mate's well rude,' Lucy said to Nathan. *'Come on Sare, let's go. Leave these losers be.*

'Hang on a minute, you can't just be like that to my friend, and then accuse me of being rude to you,' Jake said.

'Whatever,' Lucy said.

'Now you're being rude to me,' Jake said. I really wanted him to shut up before it kicked off.

'How am I?' She asked.

''Cause you are. Just 'cause I don't like you being blatantly rude to my friends, and just 'cause I don't want to go out with you, doesn't mean you can get lairy,' he said.

'Jake, what the fuck, man? These are my friends,' Nathan said.

'No, Nathan,' Jake stood up. *'We are your friends.'*

'Jake, just leave it, man,' I took his arm.

'No, I will not leave it. Didn't you just hear what she said about you? Who is that dickhead Danny, anyway? Who does he think he is to decide who's cool and who's not? I'm not having it, Ads.'

'Do you know who you're talking to?' Lucy asked.

'What's that supposed to mean?' Jake asked.

'Jake, shut up, man,' Nathan shouted.

'No, I will not shut up, Nath,' he said. His tone was short and angry. I tried to pull him away.

'Whatever, man,' Lucy said. *'But I'm tellin' you, you'll regret the day you were rude to me.'*

'Does it look like I'm scared?' Jake asked, half laughing.

'You should be,' Lucy said, before she linked her arm in Sarah's and they walked off.

'Sarah, Luce, wait up a sec,' Nathan called after them.

'What's wrong with you?' Nathan asked Jake.

'Nothing, I was just being honest.'

'I try and do a nice thing for you, man,' Nathan shook his head at Jake.

'What?' Jake twisted his face up.

'Setting you up with Lucy,' he said, like Jake was an idiot.

'I don't wanna go out with her, she's not my type,' Jake said.

'Whatever, man, can't believe how rude you were, though. And, man, you should not go shouting your mouth off about Danny, you know,' Nathan shook his head and walked after Sarah and Lucy.

'Ditching us again?' Jake called after him.

'Leave him,' I said. 'Let him go.'

Polly skidded into the front room with a huge bowl of popcorn, and jumped onto the sofa next to me.

'You want these shut?' Debbie asked, holding on to one of the curtains.

'Oh yes,' Jake said. He wiggled down onto the sofa and tucked his Power Rangers duvet in tighter around him.

'This is so exciting,' Polly said. 'I've never done anything like this before.'

'You've not lived until you've joined in Jake and Adam's Christmas Eve Movie Extravaganza, have you, Ads?' Jake asked.

'Not even a little bit.'

I smiled at Polly. She snuggled in a bit closer. I grabbed a handful of popcorn.

'Mum, hit the lights. And no snogging in the back row, you two,' Jake said.

Polly had been hanging out with us a lot the last few days, and I'd been worried Jake was feeling like a spare part. I'd asked him that morning when Debbie had invited Polly to join in the movie day. He smiled and patted me on the back. Then he told me that any girlfriend of mine had to get used to our traditions, especially the Christmas Eve Movie Extravaganza.

We were just getting to the good bit in Home Alone *when there was loads of banging on the front door.*

'Did you hear that?' Jake asked as he paused the TV.

Debbie had gone off to do some last-minute Christmas shopping, so we were the only ones in.

The banging happened again.

'You go,' Jake said to me from under his duvet.

'Why me? I'm comfortable.'

'God, you two are the laziest arseholes on the planet,' Polly sighed. 'I'll go.'

She walked down the hallway and opened the door. Nobody spoke, then the living-room door flew open and Nathan stood there with the widest eyes I'd ever seen on him.

'Your cousin ...' He pointed at Polly as she moved him out of the way and came and sat back down next to me. 'Your cousin is a mentalist.' He was out of breath.

'Tell me something I don't already know,' she sighed.

'What's happened?' Jake looked up at him. 'And also, hello. Surprised you remembered where I live.'

'Don't start,' Nathan said, moving Jake's duvet and sitting down.

'Well, what's he done then?' Polly asked.

'He got arrested.'

'What for?' I asked.

'He had a brake light out, feds pulled him over, he had weed on him.'

'Serves him right,' Jake said.

'Were you with him?' I asked.

'Yeah, I was with him and I shat my pants. I totally thought I was gonna go down with him. My mum and dad would have freaked out, man.'

'So what you gonna do?' Jake asked.

'Stay away from him innit? I can't risk it, man, if I get done for anything I can't go uni, and you don't even wanna know what my mum and dad will do if that happens.' He sighed and leant back.

'So that's it, done?' I asked.

'Totally,' he said.

'What about Sarah?' Jake asked.

'I can carry on seeing her,' Nathan said. 'I'm just not hanging around with Danny anymore, that's all.'

I looked at Jake and he shrugged. Despite what Polly and Ed had said, I wasn't expecting Nathan and Danny's love affair to be over that quickly.

'What we watching?' Nathan asked, settling himself down.

'Hang on a minute,' Jake said. 'Danny gets arrested, you shit your pants, decide it's over between the two of you, and come running back to us? Have you forgotten how much of a dickhead you've been to us both?'

Nathan stared at the wall. Then he jumped up. 'Fine,' he said and went to leave the room. 'Thanks a fucking lot,' he said.

'There's no need to get defensive,' Jake said. 'All you have to do is say you're sorry.'

Nathan put his head down. He mumbled something that resembled sorry, under his breath. 'What we watching?' He asked.

'Home Alone,' Jake said, still unimpressed, but un-pausing the TV.

We sat together watching movies for the rest of the day. The banter between us slowly came back and the atmosphere lifted.

Polly held my hand under the duvet, and it was all perfect. I wanted to suck up the happiness but I couldn't.

I still felt unsettled. Nathan wasn't just going to switch back to who he was before Danny came along. And how could he hang out with Sarah without seeing Danny? Danny wasn't the sort of person you just dump as a friend. There was no way he'd take that well. Even though Nathan was back, I couldn't shake the feeling of dread.

I was sure it wasn't over.

Eleven

I still wanted to be out of the hospital. After I'd written myself exhausted, I'd spent almost all night pacing up and down my room. I wanted to scream out in frustration, in anger; anything to get this emotion off my chest and out of my body. It was trapped in there, and it was like it was eating me up from the inside out. I couldn't deal with it, I couldn't handle it. I wanted to gouge a big hole in my chest so it could all pour out, onto the floor and away from me.

I knew writing it down would bring everything back.

I'd been sick three times in the night. I'd had the nightmare again. My head felt like someone had taken a sledgehammer to it and my heart was beating so fast. Sometimes it would flutter really strongly and I would think I was about to die. It was just like before. Just like before I took all the pills.

If I could just scream, or something ...

I needed to break into the cleaning cupboard and get the bleach, and go into the bathroom and lock myself in there somehow, so they couldn't stop me. Then I'd be gone and with Jake. That was all I wanted, to be with him. I missed him so much.

I stormed out of my room and down the corridor to the far end where the cleaning cupboard was. I kicked the door over and over again. I knew they were coming, the nurse from my room was shouting. I could hear them running towards me.

A pair of strong arms went around my waist and lifted me up, but they didn't count on the strength all that emotion was giving me and I broke free of their grip, spun around, and pushed them hard away from me.

Then there were more of them. I kicked out but they had hold of me. They carried back to my room, held me down and gave me an injection.

People were in my room. I could hear giggling. I opened my eyes slowly.

It was Blake and Josie. They were standing in my doorway. The nurse, who was sitting on a plastic chair close to my bed, smiled at them as they walked in. She didn't get up and go away though, she stayed right where she was, but pretended not to be interested in what they wanted.

'He's awake,' Josie said.

Blake's face broke into a really big smile. 'Adam,' he sang, loudly.

'Blake, use your inside voice, shhhh,' Josie rolled her eyes at me.

'We've come to cheer you up,' Blake said in a shouty whisper. 'I wrote you a poem. Wanna hear it?'

I sat up on my elbows. I wondered what time it was and how long I'd been asleep. The window in my room was letting in a little bit of daylight, so I must have slept right through.

Blake cleared his throat.

'We know you're sad and mad and–'

'Not crazy mad, mad like angry mad,' Josie said.

'Shut up and let me do the poem,' Blake said. He cleared his throat again. 'We know you're sad and mad, and that makes us sad, and we'd be glad if it weren't bad, and you got up and came to play Monopoly because Caitlin threw the board across the room and stole the doggy counter and ran off because she's mad.' He stopped. 'Mad like crazy mad.'

He looked at me, waiting for a response.

I didn't give him one.

'I know it's not much of an actual poem, but that did just happen,' he said.

'True story,' Josie said.

I wanted them to go away. I wanted to be left alone.

'OK,' Blake said, rubbing his forehead. 'If you don't want to play Monopoly, at least come and help me convince Damian to
140

go out and get us some cakes.'

'Damian's not in today, doofus,' Josie said, sitting on my bed.

'Yeah, he is, I saw him this morning.'

'No he's not.'

'Yeah he is.'

'No, he really isn't. It's Anna today.'

'Who's Anna?' Blake asked. He was fidgeting from foot to foot and he looked like he was going to cry.

'The old nurse,' Josie turned to me. 'She's the dragon one.'

'No, it's Damian,' Blake said. 'I'm gonna go and find him, and get him to come in, then you'll be wrong, and you'll have to say sorry.' He left the room.

'You OK?' Josie asked me.

I shook my head.

'You missed breakfast and group therapy,' she said. 'David said he was letting you sleep as they said you'd been up all night after the thing with the cupboard last night.'

I didn't want her in my room. I wanted to be left alone but I knew she wasn't going anywhere, so I got up and walked out and away from her. My brain didn't want to think, or listen to anyone, or do anything at all. Staring at a wall or just sleeping were all I was capable of. I didn't want to see or speak to anyone.

I went to the rec room. There were people in there. Caitlin was shouting and Blake was running around, panicked, looking for Damian.

'Come outside for a fag when we go down,' Josie said, appearing behind me.

I could feel the panic. The noises on the ward were ten times louder in my head than they should have been, amplified, but also muffled like I was under water.

'Are you OK, Adam?' Someone said. I don't know who.

Everything went blurry, like my eyes wouldn't work, and my heart was racing, sweat was pouring down my forehead.

'Blake, he's not in,' someone said and Blake started crying.

'Blake, shut up,' that was Caitlin, I think.

I felt sick. Then I heard Jake's voice. I heard it. In among all the noises on the ward, in among all the shouting, crying, and laughing that was so loud, I heard him. I'd know it anywhere.

'Adam'. That was all he said. Just my name. Like he was shouting it from a distance, calling me over.

I sat on a chair. There was a hand on my back but I don't know whose it was. I was shaking. The nausea was getting worse. I tried to breathe it away but it didn't work. I was sick on the floor, and Caitlin screamed, and people moved quickly then David was there. He held me up as he walked me back to my room, only stopping when I heaved again.

I couldn't see straight. I couldn't think straight. I didn't know what was happening to me, or how to make it stop.

David sat me on my bed, grabbed the chair, and sat opposite me. He was telling me to breathe, just to breathe slowly, but I couldn't.

'I need a screen up, now,' he said to the nurse who'd followed us in. 'And Caitlin, Josie, Blake, please leave us alone now.'

I looked up and all three of them were standing in the corridor looking in, really worried. I caught Josie's eye and she was about to cry, I could tell.

'Now,' David said – and they went.

Then he turned back to me and was telling me to breathe slowly again, and showing me how he wanted me to do it.

'It's OK,' he said, when I'd caught my breath.

The nurse handed me a cup of water and told me to sip slowly. David told her to leave the room, but to stay just outside in case he needed her. Then he made me lie down on my bed, but propped up by the pillows. We sat there for a while; until he was sure I'd calmed down.

I wanted to tell him that I'd heard Jake; I wanted to ask him what was wrong with me, and how to make it stop, but I couldn't. I felt weak and woozy; I was sort of drifting in and out of sleep while he sat and read through what I'd written down in my pad.

'Are you feeling like this because the next thing that you've got to write about is the day it happened?' He said in a really soft voice.

I turned away from him because I didn't want to answer, and

I was still feeling angry, because I was stuck in there with no way out.

'Are you hungry?' he asked. 'Do you want some toast to settle your stomach?'

I shook my head.

'Adam, can you turn and look at me a moment?'

I moved my whole body round to face him.

'What if I was to tell you that I already know what happened that night and what you did?'

My whole body tensed up.

'It's OK,' he said. 'What if I was to point out to you that Josie tells me she knows, yet all I see is her desperately wanting you to be her friend?'

I started shaking.

'And what if I also point out that Polly knows, too? And she thinks the world of you Adam, she really does.'

I closed my eyes against him, against the world. What he'd said about Josie and Polly might have been true; but not only did I question their motives, it was also completely overridden by the fact that Debbie didn't want to know me. Not only that, it was one thing them being able to forgive me, but I knew I'd never be able to forgive myself.

David was looking at me with a strange expression, maybe pity, sympathy, or concern, or maybe all three rolled into one.

'But the important thing is that I know, but I need to hear your interpretation of it. Only then can I help you get better, Adam.' He sat forward and put his hand on my shoulder. 'I can make all of this stop – the nightmares, the panic, the trauma – but I need you to tell me what happened first.'

I wanted to speak then. It was like I wanted to pour it all out of my mouth quickly and furiously. It was like it had been sitting in my guts, festering, going mouldy and rancid, and at that moment, I wanted it out.

I tried to speak.

David sat up straight. 'Can you?' He asked.

It wouldn't come out and I shook my head.

'Do you trust me when I say I'm not going to let anything bad happen to you while you're here? You don't need to be afraid,' he said.

I thought back to how he'd been with me since I got here. If what he said was true, then maybe he didn't think I was scum of the earth for what I did. Or maybe he did and it was just his job to make me better. Maybe I was just another statistic. If he got me well and out again, maybe he'd get a bonus.

'Have I let you down so far?' He asked. It scared me that he always seemed to know what I was thinking.

It had come back to the fact that I didn't have a lot of choice, and I guessed I could get as angry about that as I liked, or I could put my trust in this man in front of me, and get on with what he'd asked me to do. One was going to get me out of there. The other was a hopeless cause.

He handed me my pad and pen. 'I'm going to stay right here while you do it. I'm not going anywhere. What I want you to do, if at any moment you don't feel safe, is to hand me back the pad and we'll stop, OK?'

I nodded. Then I started writing.

I woke up in my own bed for once. Polly wasn't with me. I'd asked her to go home, because I was so nervous about the fact we'd probably end up having sex if she stayed. I know it might sound ridiculous, but I didn't feel like I was ready to. Not yet. She'd said she was OK about it but it was still playing on my mind. Now she'd gone away for New Year's and it was going to torture me until she got back, I knew it.

'What's the matter with you, grumpy shit?' My dad asked when I walked into the kitchen and put the kettle on.

I ignored him. I didn't want to talk to him.

'What happened to that girl that was here last night then?' He asked, getting a Sterling out of his packet and lighting it. The ashtray next to him was overflowing already. I wondered how long he'd been up, and why he was even here, and not down the bookies or the pub.

'She went home,' I said.

'Did you fuck her?'

'Dad ... Jesus.'

'I'll have a coffee if you're making one.'

I got another mug out of the cupboard.

'So, what you up to tonight, then? You got a party to go to or anything?'

I turned around and leant on the counter while I waited for the kettle to boil. 'Yeah, there's a party down The Shed, under eighteens.'

He laughed. 'You going with Jake and Nath?'

'Yep,' I said. The kettle clicked and I turned round to make the drinks.

'He's not hanging around with that Danny anymore, then?'

'How do you know about that?' I asked, as I got the milk out of the almost empty fridge.

'Debbie rang me up and told me about it, said to keep an eye on things as she don't like the sound of him, said he'd got arrested or something?'

'Yeah, he had weed on him.'

'Are you doing drugs?' He stubbed his fag out in the overflowing ashtray and opened his paper.

'No,' I said, putting his coffee down next to him.

'Good,' he said, without looking up. 'Cor, she's got nice tits.' He said pointing at the naked woman on page three.

'Dad, please,' I said. I went to walk out the kitchen with my cup of tea.

'Ads, hang up,' he said. He stood up and reached into his back pocket and pulled out a fiver. 'Get some chips or something, cupboards are bare again.'

I took it off him. 'Thanks,' I said.

'Jackie and I are in tonight,' he said as I walked out of the room. That explained the fiver. Bribery. Stay out the way. Don't come home.

Not that I'd want to. Every time I saw that woman, I wanted to punch her in the face.

I went to the park via the chicken shop with the fiver Dad gave me. When I got there, Nathan and Jake were sitting on our bench.

'Are you, my boys, ready for the New Year's Eve of all New Year's Eves?' I asked them.

They looked at each other, then Nathan looked at the floor, and Jake looked at me and shrugged.

'What?'

'I couldn't get the tickets,' Nathan said, still looking at the floor.

'What? You're joking, why not?' I asked him.

'My mum didn't leave me the cash,' he said. He got up and picked the football up. I sat down in his place.

'What are we gonna do now?' I asked him.

'We'll find something,' Jake said, but I could hear how upset he was. He was looking forward to going out on the pull. He'd decided he was over Kelly and ready to fall in love again, and tonight would be the night.

Nathan kept quiet. He sat down next to me, taking his phone out of his pocket as he did.

'When did you get that smart-looking piece of flash?'

'For Christmas, innit, but it only came this morning,' Nathan said.

'What's that game?' Jake asked as something colourful

146

flashed up on the screen.

'Candy Crush,'

'iPhone 5?' I asked him.

'Oh yes,' Nathan said.

'Show off.' Jake got up, and kicked the ball out from under Nathan's feet and picked it up.

'You're just jealous 'cause your Nokia could build a house,' Nathan said. He leant in and took a handful of my chips. 'You eating out again?'

'Yeah, no food in the house at all.

'We've told you before, you'll get fat eating that shit all day long,' Jake said.

'Yeah, then Polly will ditch you for being a fat bloater.' Nathan laughed.

'Never,' Jake said. He was smiling at me, a knowing smile, and it made me feel warm. He liked Polly a lot. He'd said she wasn't for him, but she was perfect for me, and he'd convinced himself that we'd be one of those couples who, in twenty years' time, have a nice house in the countryside with four kids, three dogs, two rabbits, and a goldfish. He said he'd be round every weekend with his supermodel girlfriend and their adopted baby, which they adopted because she didn't want to lose her figure. He'd painted this massive picture in his head and I'd told him he was mad, but actually, I loved it.

'So how's Sarah, have you heard from her?' I asked Nathan. He'd been with us pretty much all week, apart from Christmas Day when his mum had dragged him back home for family stuff. I didn't think he'd have had the time to see her in among all of that. He definitely hadn't seen Danny, and that was the biggest relief on the planet.

'Yeah, she's OK,' he said.

'So you have heard from her,' I asked.

'Yeah, a bit,' he said. He was being shifty; I could tell by the tone of his voice.

Jake stopped kicking the ball. 'How's the sexy time going?' He asked.

Nathan laughed. 'I'm not telling you anything,' he said.

'What? You told us everything with Megan. You won't tell us

anything about Sarah,' I said. 'Why not?'

'I don't want you opening your big traps later,' he said, and he stood up and put his hands in his pockets.

'Later?' I asked.

'Go on,' Jake said.

'Yeah, I thought we might go to Danny's house party,' he said.

'Danny's house party?' I asked. Jake's jaw was on the floor. I shook my head and he shrugged.

'Is this why you didn't get the tickets for The Shed?' Jake asked. He was pissed off. I was pissed off, too. It made sense now.

'You didn't get the tickets on purpose so we could go to Danny's.' I said.

'No,' Nathan said in a properly snappy voice.

'Don't get shitty, man,' Jake said.

'I'm not.'

'I thought you were done with him?' I asked.

Nathan shrugged.

'So is this about Sarah being there, or is this about you not being able to stay away from Danny?' I asked.

'You've not mentioned him for a week. How comes suddenly you're ditching our plans to go to his party?'

'I'm not ditching our plans, I told you my mum didn't leave the money.' He was almost shouting. 'And I don't know what your problem is with Danny, both of you. I'm getting sick of it.'

'Erm, aren't we forgetting him getting arrested?' I asked.

Nobody said anything. Nathan sat back down on the bench and got his phone out. The tension was huge. It was believable Nathan's parents might have forgotten, but there was something inside me that didn't buy his story.

'You're a sly bastard,' Jake said.

'Don't fucking start,' Nathan said. 'Look, whatever, come if you want, or not – you lot are pissing me off. I'm gone.' Nathan picked up his ball from under Jake's foot and stormed off.

Jake sat down next to me and neither of us said anything for a while. I felt like I'd been punched in the stomach. I really thought that we'd heard the last of Danny, but clearly not. It was starting again. I didn't like it.

'What we gonna do?' Jake asked.

'I think we should go,' I said.

'Because you wanna prove a point to Nath, or because you actually wanna spend New Year's Eve at Danny's shit-hole having your eardrums ruptured by his shit music?'

'No, because I want to spend New Year's Eve with Nathan, like we do every year,' I said, and it was the truth. I was furious but I reckoned the best thing to do would be to go, make an effort, try and all get along. It was the only way we'd be able to see the new year in together.

It'd been three hours since we'd left the park, and Jake was still harping on like an old woman about how we'd been duped by Nathan. I wanted to take the pillow out from behind my back and smother him with it, because I thought it was the only thing that would shut him up.

'He's such a slimy arse. I don't believe him, you know, I don't believe him one bit that his mum and dad didn't leave him the money for the tickets,' he said.

'I know, you've said a thousand times already.'

We were playing FIFA on the Xbox and I knew how pissed off he was, because I was winning. I'd never won a game of FIFA in all our sixteen years.

'I reckon he just wanted to go to Danny's party, you know, but he didn't have the balls to say it.'

'Just chill out, man. It'll be OK, we'll have a good time.'

'Your attitude has changed,' he said, taking the giant bag of crisps off my lap. 'You actually want to go to this party?'

'If he's gonna be friends with Danny, he's gonna be friends with Danny, right?'

'Yeah, but that doesn't mean we have to be friends with Danny.' Jake made a face.

'No, but if we wanna spend New Year with Nathan, we have to go.'

'To Danny's house party? Ad, you know how much I hate house parties.'

I laughed.

'Why you laughing?'

'One bad experience and it puts you off for life.'

He threw the Xbox controller down on the bed and put his hands on his head.

'I really wanted to go to The Shed for New Year's, man. There was gonna be some fitness there, you know, I could feel it in my bones.'

'There might be at Danny's? What about Lucy? You know how she feels about you,' I couldn't hold back my laughter.

Jake exhaled about four lungs worth of air in one go. 'Apparently, I'm gonna regret the day I was rude to her or something.'

'Dinner,' Debbie's voice came shouting up the stairs.

'Come on, let's eat and get ready. We wanna spend New Year with Nathan, don't we?' I asked.

'S'pose,' he said.

Jake wouldn't snap out of his strop the whole way there, even though I was trying to cheer him up. I felt nervous as we walked over to Danny's, like we were about to walk into a lion's den or something. It didn't help that Polly had told me I was mental for wanting to go, and finished the phone call by telling me good luck. She'd gone up north, under duress, with her mum and dad and Ed for New Year. If she was around, I would have made her come with us just to make things a bit easier. She seemed to have a knack with Danny. She didn't take his attitude.

When we got there, the front door was open and I made Jake go in first.

'Just go and find Nathan,' I said when he hesitated.

The place was packed and the music was blaring. The atmosphere was the complete opposite of Ed's party. It wasn't friendly. I wanted to turn and run the other way, admit defeat, and let Nathan get on with it with Danny.

Nathan was in the kitchen.

'Came then?' He asked in a pissed-off tone. He wasn't pleased to see us.

'Looks like it,' Jake said in his properly sarcastic voice.

'No need to be sarky.'

'No need to be an arsehole.'

'You two are doing my head in already,' I said. 'Stop it; let's just have fun, yeah? Is Sarah alright?' I asked. It was the only thing I could think of that would lighten the mood.

Nathan looked out into the big room off the kitchen. She stood next to Danny at a mixing deck in the corner. She was all dressed up and looked really nice.

'Yeah, she's fiiiine,' he said. He smiled at her and I waved.

Jake didn't move or say anything. His face was like stone.

'Go home if you don't like it,' Nathan said to him.

'I just don't know what you see in these people?'

'Fuck off, Jake, these are my friends.'

'No, we are your friends,' he said.

Nathan laughed. 'I can't help it if you're getting jealous of my new life. I can't hang around with you losers forever, can I?' He patted Jake on the back.

'Nath, man,' I said.

He stopped laughing. 'I'm kidding alright. Keep your tits on, and try and have a good time,' he said. He walked over to Sarah and gave her a kiss.

'Wanker,' Jake said when he was gone.

'Look, man, I know you love him but just leave off a bit tonight, yeah?' I asked.

'Why should I? He's being a dick.'

'I just don't want it kicking off, I hate it when we argue, can't we just be nice?' I smiled my cheesiest smile at him.

He didn't smile back.

'To be honest, Ad, I feel well out of place. I'd rather be at home drinking tea with my mum and watching bloody Eastenders, and that's saying something.'

I laughed; then stopped because Danny was next to Jake. He'd appeared out of nowhere.

'Nobody asked you to come,' he said. His face was cold and hard.

Neither of us said anything. I tried to remember what Polly had told me about him – that he just thinks he's hard, and that he's harmless really.

'What? Cat got your tongue?' He asked.

'Thanks for the invite, Danny,' Jake said and held his drink up to him in a mock toast.

'I didn't invite you, Nathan did.'

He was making me nervous.

'Oh well,' Jake said. I wanted him to stop being sarcastic and just leave it. 'Thanks to Nathan, then.' Jake raised his glass in Nathan's direction.

'Bit of advice,' Danny said.

Oh God. 'Go on,' I said.

'Stop being such losers. Nath is cool and you're holding him back.'

Jake's back straightened and his chest puffed out. I knew something bad was about to come out of his mouth and I braced myself for it.

'Fuck you,' he said. A bit of spit came out of his mouth.

I wanted to run and hide under the table, but I was brave.

'Look, we're all friends here,' I said.

Danny looked at me but his face didn't move. 'No we're not,' he said. He turned to Jake. 'I heard about you shouting off in the park about me, and about you disrespecting my friend Lucy. It's stuff like that I don't like.' He held Jake's gaze for what felt like a lifetime, then he went back off into his party, leaving me to wonder if I had actually just shat myself.

Before I could say or do anything else, Jake stormed off, and I followed him out of the front door, into the bitter night air.

We were on our park bench. It was freezing cold and drizzling. I was fed up. It was half eleven and we had nowhere to be for midnight. I was annoyed with Jake. All I'd been trying to do was keep the peace, to try and get everyone to relax and have fun, but it had completely backfired and our evening was ruined. I was getting to the point where I was sure the only option left was to stop fighting for Nathan. I was thinking that maybe, the more you fight, the more you end up pushing them away. Maybe we just had to let him go.

Jake sighed.

'What?'

'Fed up, man, this is shit. Let's just go.'

'Where?'

'Yours, 'cause my mum's in.'

'My dad's in.'

'Fuck's sake,' he said, and crossed his arms, sulking like a little toddler.

'I don't know why you had to start,' I said to him. I couldn't hold it in. 'I don't get why you couldn't have just left it?'

'So it's my fault now?'

'Did I say that?'

'Sounds like it.'

'Jeez, you can be such a woman sometimes.'

'Shut up,' he said, and I did because otherwise we'd just get into a big argument.

I knew he didn't want to lose Nathan either but I was pissed off with him for not keeping his mouth shut. If he had we might still have been there, maybe even enjoying ourselves a bit, and not sitting on our bench, on our lonesome, in the rain, freezing our bollocks off with nowhere to go.

I heard the park gate creek open in the distance.

I squinted over to see what looked like a crowd of people coming over our way.

I sat up straight on the bench and leant forwards to try and see more clearly through the darkness.

'Who's that?' Jake asked, leaning forwards too.

'Dunno,' I said. 'Looks like they're coming over.'

When they crossed one of the paths lit by street lamps, I saw it was Nathan and Danny. Sarah and Lucy were there too, and a load of others.

I stood up straight away. So did Jake.

'What the fuck?' He said.

Something didn't feel right.

When they got close enough for me to see Nathan's face, my stomach jumped because he looked so angry.

I took a step towards him but he walked straight past me, straight up to Jake and got straight in his face.

'Where's my fucking phone?' he spat.

'Don't let him take the piss, Nath, teach him,' Danny said.

'What? Nathan? Jake?' The words were coming out of my mouth, but they weren't listening to me.

They were squared up to each other. Staring into each other's eyes.

Sarah came out of the crowd with wide eyes. She grabbed Nathan's arm and tried to pull him away. He brushed her off.

'I said, where's my fucking phone?'

'Look, just calm down, yeah? What's going on?' I asked.

Sarah tried to pull Nathan away again. 'I think we should just leave it. I don't want you to fight.'

'Just stay out of it,' Danny said.

Lucy appeared and pulled Sarah away. 'Yeah, leave them, man,' she said. 'If they wanna fight like little kids, let them do it.'

They weren't going to fight. It was just a stupid misunderstanding. They were friends. It was ridiculous.

They were staring at each other. Their gazes steady. The crowd was circling.

My heart raced. 'Nathan, what the hell is going on?'

'This twat has nicked my phone,' he said to me, still staring at Jake. 'She saw him with it.' He was pointing at Lucy.

'Whoa,' Lucy said. 'I didn't say he definitely had it, I just said–'

'Why you back tracking?' Danny cut in.

'I'm not, I'm just saying.'

'Just stay out of it, yeah. It's between him and Jake.'

My head darted from Danny, to Lucy, to Jake, to Nathan.

'Nath?'

'Leave it,' Danny warned me.

I tried to grab Nathan and pull him away. Danny stepped between us and spun me around by the shoulders. His cold gaze didn't move as he punched me hard in the stomach, winding me.

While I tried to catch my breath, he pushed me to the floor. He straddled over me, holding me down. When I struggled he pinned me down harder, pushing my shoulders down into the wet grass.

'I said, leave it.' His face was close and I could smell the beer on his breath.

154

He turned to Nathan. 'Teach him, Nath,' he said. Then he turned his face back to mine and raised his eyebrows in a smile.

'Get off me,' I said, but he wasn't letting go.

Jake backed off to walk away, but the crowd pushed him back. He lost his footing, put his arms out to steady himself, and accidentally pushed Nathan.

Nathan punched Jake straight in the stomach.

'Nathan, stop it,' I shouted. I was desperate. 'Get off me,' I spat at Danny but he held me down harder.

Then the crowd went mental, the noise was insane. The shouting, jeering, cheering. Jake and Nathan were having a full-on fight. I couldn't believe what I was seeing. I couldn't believe what was happening. I used all my strength to try and get up and stop them, to stop the madness. Jake didn't have his phone. Why would Lucy say that? I tried so hard to get up, but I couldn't. Danny was too strong for me.

Nathan took a swing for Jake's leg, and I thought it was a really strange place for him to go for.

He stopped and walked backwards, away from Jake.
The crowd went quiet and backed away, too. The electricity in the air had been replaced with a thick, dense tension.

Danny's face changed. He released the pressure and jumped up. 'What the fuck?' He said.

Nathan stood, rigid, looking at the Stanley knife in his hand.

My whole body exploded in terror and I was up, and at Jake's side.

I helped him to the bench.

He wasn't talking.

I pulled his hand away from his thigh and he screamed. He was bleeding badly.

Nathan had stabbed him.

He'd stabbed Jake.

Adrenalin took over and I launched myself at Nathan, punching him in the chest over and over again. He didn't move. He didn't even look at me. He was just staring at Jake.

Sarah was crying, and screaming, and pushing him. 'What have you done, Nath?'

Lucy stood at the edge of the crowd with her hand over her mouth.

Danny was standing with his hands on his head. The colour had drained from his face. 'What the fuck have you done?' He said.

Nathan and Jake's eyes were locked on to each other.

'Put the knife away, man,' Danny said. 'We need to get out of here.' He turned to the crowd. 'Go,' he shouted.

They all ran off, fast, in different directions.

'Nath, come on,' Danny said. When Nathan didn't move, Danny shook his head. He got up close in his face. 'If you go down for this, don't you dare take me down with you.'

Nathan's head snapped towards Danny. 'You told me to teach him,' he whispered.

'Did I tell you to stab him?' Danny asked. 'No. Now let's get the fuck out of here before the feds turn up.' Danny ran off, shouting for Nathan to catch him up.

Nathan put the blade of the knife away, and put it in his pocket. He looked at me, then back to Jake, but there was no emotion in his face.

'We need to go,' he said.

'We can't just leave him here,' Sarah was crying hysterically.

'Sarah, Adam, let's go,' he said.

'What's wrong with you? We can't leave him here,' I said.

'He'll be fine. It's just his leg. Let's go,' he said. He pulled me by the arm and we started to move.

I stopped. Jake was sitting on the bench holding his leg. He looked up at me. His face was full of pain and fear.

'Come on, Adam,' Nathan shouted back. 'Come on, he'll be OK.'

I was full of panic. I couldn't breathe.

Nathan ran back towards me. He grabbed my arm. 'Come on,' he said. 'He'll be fine, he's gonna limp home to Debbie and she's gonna put a plaster on it. Come on.' He shook my arm.

I looked back at Jake.

I heard a siren in the distance.

'Come on, you two,' Sarah shouted.

The siren was getting louder. Nathan and I looked at each other, nodded, then legged it out the park as fast as we could.

Dad collared me the second I walked through the front door.

'Where the fucking hell have you been?' He screamed from the kitchen doorway. He was standing in just his jeans. His hair was a mess. His face was angry red.

I froze on the spot.

'What happened to Jake?' He asked.

'What?' I tried to work out how long it had been since I left Nathan. Half an hour at the most. Long enough for Jake to hobble home and for Debbie to call my dad.

'What happened to him?' He asked.

'I don't know,' I said.

'Don't lie to me,' my dad spat.

'I'm not.'

'Don't fucking lie to me,' he was shouting loudly.

I took a step back. He took one forwards.

'Where is he? What happened?'

'I don't know. I honestly don't know. Last time I saw him he was–'

'He was lying in the park unconscious?'

My blood ran cold. It couldn't be. I knew it wasn't right. There was no way ...

'You heard me.'

'Unconscious? But–'

'Now tell me what the fuck happened.' Dad was right up in my face.

He was demanding to know what had gone on, but I couldn't think straight. I couldn't stop the panic enough to tell him. I pushed past him.

'I need to see him,' I said. 'I need to see him. How was he unconscious, Dad? How do you know? How do you know that?'

He grabbed me by the hood of my parka jacket. 'Because I've just had a frantic Debbie on the phone, wanting to know why the hell some random stranger has just answered Jake's phone and said there were paramedics there, and she couldn't talk to him because he was unconscious, and they were rushing

157

him straight to hospital.' He stopped and caught his breath. 'Now tell me what the fuck happened.'

My legs went weak. I walked to the kitchen, pulled out a chair, and sat down. Paramedics. A stranger. He was unconscious. It didn't make any sense.

'It all happened so fast,' I said.

Dad's hands came down on the table in front of me so hard, and he shouted in my ear so loudly, I jumped. 'Tell me what happened.'

'There was a fight, that's all.'

'What happened to his leg?'

I looked up at him.

'Adam, I haven't got time for this. Tell me what happened to his leg. Debbie is doing her fucking nut with worry.'

'He was stabbed,' I said, but it barely came out.

'Oh my fucking God,' Dad said backing away and putting his hands on his head. He stopped. 'Not by you, please God, not by you?' He was pointing at me.

'No.'

'Who?'

'I don't know.'

'Don't lie to me, Adam. Don't fucking lie to me.'

'Nathan did it.'

'Nathan?'

'Is Jake OK?' I asked. I wanted to get up and go and find him at the hospital. I needed to say sorry. I needed to make sure he was OK.

'Nathan?' Dad was saying over and over again. 'Jesus Christ, Jesus fucking Christ.'

I stood up. 'I need to get to the hospital, I need to see him,' I said.

He ignored me, barged past me into the hallway and picked up the phone.

'What are you doing?' I asked him from the kitchen doorway.

'Calling the police,' he said. His voice was calm now.

I flew down the hallway so fast and tried to grab the phone from him. 'You can't, Dad. You can't.'

'I can and I bloody will,' he said. 'This is serious, Adam. Fucking serious.'

'Dad, I just need to see Jake. Please drive me to the hospital,' I pleaded with him.

He looked right into my eyes. He put the phone down. 'I can't,' he said. 'I'm over the limit.'

That was it, I grabbed the front door handle, and went to open it, but he pulled me back.

'Where are you going?' He asked.

'To find Jake.'

He picked the phone back up again. 'Dad, don't. Let me see him first,' I said.

'I'm calling a cab,' he said.

'I'm waiting outside,' I said.

I stood in the drizzling rain and tried to work out in my head how Jake had ended up unconscious. There must have been a mistake. He was stabbed in the leg. There was no way that would have made him unconscious. Maybe he'd just fainted or something. That wasn't serious. He'd be OK. He'd be sitting up in one of the cubicles when I got there, flirting with the nurses and giving me evil, pissed-off looks for leaving him there.

I was going to have some serious grovelling to do.

I jumped out of the cab, leaving my dad to pay, and ran into A&E out of breath.

'Jake Coldridge,' I said to the receptionist.

She came out from behind her desk. 'This way,' she said.

She walked me through some doors and down a busy corridor to a private waiting room.

Debbie was sitting on a chair.

'Oh my God, Adam,' she ran over and grabbed my shoulders. 'What happened? Please tell me, what happened to Jake?' Her face was so full of anguish. She must have rushed to the hospital; she was in her pyjamas with a jacket over the top.

'There was a fight. Where is he?' I asked.

'Please God, no,' she said. 'What happened, Adam? Please tell me?'

'Him and Nathan,' I said.

'Nathan?' She stepped back. 'No, I won't believe it, not our Nathan.'

There was such a bad feeling in the room; the air was thick with worry. I just wanted to know where Jake was. I couldn't understand why Debbie wasn't with him, and why they hadn't taken me straight to him.

'I'm sorry, Debbie. It was a bad fight, really bad,' I told her.

'What, why? Why?' She was pacing and it was making me nervous.

'I don't know. Where is Jake?' I asked.

'I don't know, they haven't told me anything.'

The door opened. We both jumped and our heads shot round. It wasn't Jake. It was the woman from reception bringing my dad in.

'Did you tell her?' He asked.

'Tell me what?'

Debbie was waiting for me to speak. My dad was glaring at me, waiting for me to tell her.

I said nothing. I couldn't.

'Look, Debbie, Nathan stabbed Jake in the leg. I think that's what Adam wanted to tell you. I'm really sorry.'

Debbie shook her head. 'I won't believe it. I can't believe it. Is this true?' She asked. I'd never seen her like this before. She looked terrified.

She was waiting for me to answer.

I nodded.

She sat down. Then she shot back up and started pacing. 'But it was just his leg, though. He'll be OK? He will be OK. Just some stitches, they're just stitching him up now, aren't they? That's why they've not come out?' She looked at us. 'Right?'

My dad sat her back down, and held her hand, but he didn't take his eyes off me.

'I'm sorry,' was all I could say.

'Where is Nathan?' She asked.

'I don't know, we ...'

'You what?' Dad asked.

'We left. I left him there. I left Jake there. So did Nathan. He *said Jake would be OK. I panicked.'*

A wail came from Debbie and my dad shook his head at me.

'That's why he was on his own. Oh my God, this is not happening.' She started crying. 'Why haven't they come out and said he's OK?'

I went to walk out the room. I couldn't just sit there and do nothing. I had to go and find him; find out what was happening.

'Don't you think about going anywhere. The police will want to talk to you. I called them when I was getting out the cab,' Dad said.

'The police?' Debbie looked at my dad in horror.

'Deb, this is serious,' he says.

'Jake will be fine, they'll make up,' she said.

'Debbie, Nathan stabbed Jake in the leg.'

She put her head in her hands. 'I can't believe it,' she said over and over again.

We fell into a suffocating silence. I walked up and down, struggling to breathe. It was like someone had sucked all the air out of the room. With each second that passed, the tension got worse. I didn't know if I should sit down, stand up, pace, cry, scream, or go to the toilet and throw up.

And every time the door opened, we all jumped up like there were springs in our feet. Was it going to be Jake? Was it going to be a nurse with news?

It was neither this time, it was a girl in a nice outfit like she'd been out clubbing. She was older than us, maybe in her twenties. She had mascara running down her face. She told me her name was Amy and she was the one who found Jake there. I had so many questions for her, but I couldn't bring myself to ask – it was like I was protecting myself from the truth: that it was a lot more serious than I'd thought.

'Why were they fighting?' Debbie asked. Her voice cut through the silence.

'Nathan thought Jake took his phone.'

'So he stabbed him in the leg?' Dad asked.

'It happened so quickly, we didn't even know until ...'

'Why would Jake take his phone?' Debbie asked.

'He didn't, Nathan just thought he did.'

'Did that Danny boy have something to do with it?' Dad stood up.

'Dad, please,' I said.

'Well, since Nath's been hanging around with him—'

'How would you know what goes on with us? You're never home and you never listen,' I was fuming with him. He couldn't just come in acting like he knew everything and start bossing me around and that.

'I'm here now, ain't I?' He said.

'Yeah, left Jackie at home in bed though?'

'What's she got to do with it?' His voice was raised and I didn't like it.

'It's got everything to do with it,' I shouted back at him.

'Look, just shut up, both of you,' Debbie stood up between us. 'I want to know what's going on with my son, not listen to your arguments.'

So we went back to the suffocating silence again.

The door opened and we all stood up. A man in trousers and a shirt walked in. He had a hospital name tag on and one of those hand gel things attached to his belt.

'Mrs Coldridge?' He looked at Debbie.

'Yes,' she said, but her words were so quiet and scared I could hardly hear her.

I looked at his face for clues. My heart seemed to have stopped inside my chest. It had stopped beating and I had stopped breathing.

'Why don't you take a seat?' He said to Debbie.

'No, just tell me what's happening with my son. Is he OK now?'

The doctor took Debbie by the arm. 'I'm sorry, I'm really sorry, we did everything we could to try and save your son—'

'Save him?' I asked. That was the strangest thing for him to say.

'Shut up, Adam,' Dad said.

The doctor carried on. 'He suffered a stab wound to the leg. When he arrived here, he'd lost a considerable amount of blood. The knife severed his femoral artery and we did everything we could, but we ...'

I stopped listening.

I swallowed down the sick from the back of my throat.

Debbie's screams tore right through me.

My legs gave way underneath me and I fell to the floor, gasping for breath.

Jake was dead.

Oh my God, he was dead.

There was a thin curtain separating me and Jake, and I was scared. I didn't want to open it because he was on the other side and he was dead.

I stood there, staring at it, still in shock. I wondered what he'd look like, if he'd started to go a funny colour. Would his lips be blue? Would they have closed his eyes?

My dad's hand was on the small of my back. 'Go on, son,' he said, but I didn't want to. All the time I didn't see him, I could pretend it wasn't real. I could pretend in my head that they'd got the wrong person, and it wasn't him, and he was at home in bed wondering where we all were.

I knew it wasn't true. Debbie had already been in to see him, and her screams could have brought down the walls of the hospital.

My hand shook so hard as I put it forward to feel for the gap in the curtain.

I put my head down and closed my eyes.

'I don't think I can do it,' I said, and turned away.

'It's up to you,' Dad said.

I'd never seen a dead body before, not a real one, only on the TV. I felt sick but I needed to see him. I needed to make sure it was him before I spoke to the police and told them everything that happened.

I pulled back the curtain. I lifted my head up and there he was. He was lying on the bed like he was asleep, but I knew he wasn't because he slept on his front with one leg out of the covers – not on his back with his arms straight.

My legs buckled; my dad held me up and helped me walk nearer.

There were no signs on him to say he was injured, but I

163

knew that beneath the thin sheet and blanket, there was a single stab wound to his leg ... A stab wound that killed him.

He was still. His chest wasn't rising and falling and he wasn't snoring. I wanted so much for him to open his eyes and smile at me. I wanted a nurse to come in and tell me I could help take his temperature, like the time he was in hospital when we were younger.

He didn't open his eyes. He didn't smile at me. I was staring at him, but he wasn't moving.

'You OK?' Dad asked. He was looking at Jake, too.

I counted backwards three hours, to when we were sitting on the bench before the fight happened, and I remembered him thinking I was blaming him for starting trouble. I was suddenly worried he still thought that. I worried he died thinking I blamed him.

I didn't.

I blamed Nathan.

Bile rose up in my throat and I swallowed it down. I wasn't sure if my brain was registering what was in front of me, because there was no way it could be true. There was no way he could be there one minute and gone the next. It didn't work like that.

But he wasn't moving. He still wasn't moving.

I was brave. I walked forward and took his hand.

'I'm sorry,' I whispered to him. I wanted to speak more, but the emotion took over and I couldn't breathe.

I fell into my dad's arms and he carried me out of the cubicle. When we got outside, my legs gave way and I collapsed in a heap on the floor.

If I hadn't left him there, I could have saved his life.

My best friend was dead and it was my fault.

Twelve

It had been two days since I'd finally got out what happened that night, and I'd only left my room to go to the toilet. I wasn't well enough. My head was still spinning, not just mentally but physically, too. My brain felt like a waltzer car that wouldn't stop. It was just going round, and round, and round. It was making me feel dizzy and sick; it didn't matter if I was sitting down, lying down, standing up, walking, pacing up and down, up and down – it wouldn't stop.

I spent most of the time curled up on the floor in a ball, crying, desperate for my thoughts to leave me alone.

Every time I closed my eyes I saw Jake's face. It wasn't his happy face, it was his face the last time I saw it when it was begging me not to leave him.

I couldn't make it go away. I could see the blood, pouring out of his leg, and the life pouring out of him.

If I had known he was going to die, I wouldn't have left him there.

I would have stayed and saved his life.

There was no escape from what was going on in my head. It was too late. I'd crossed the line. There were no stolen fag breaks, games of pool, or late-night storm watching. It was just me and my thoughts, in my room, being watched by whichever nurse was sent to supervise me.

I knew I was going crazy and it terrified me. Every now and again I'd stop being scared and I'd get angry instead. Angry with my dad for putting me in the hospital, angry with David for making me tell him what happened, angry with Nathan for stabbing Jake in the leg and killing him.

I knew things were critical when I heard Jake's voice again.

Not in my head, I actually heard it. Like he was standing in the room with me.

(A whisper): Why did you leave me, Adam?

Go away. Please go away.

(Angry shouting): Why did you leave me there to die?

No, no, leave me alone, no.

(Calm): It's all your fault.

I'm sorry, I'm sorry, I'm sorry.

I covered my face with the blanket. I didn't want to see his ghost, I couldn't, I didn't, I couldn't, I–

(Angry): Why did you leave me, Adam? Why did you leave me? Why did you leave me?

Stop! Stop! I'm sorry. I'm sorry.

I couldn't breathe. I was choking, gasping, spluttering everywhere. I didn't know what was happening. I thought I was dying, too.

They came running into the room and gave me an injection.

I fell asleep.

But he was there when I woke. He was there leaning on the sink, with his arms folded across his chest, and he was staring at me.

No. No – go away. I'm sorry, just go away.

(His voice was calm, he started with a sigh): You know, my mum lied to us, when she said there was a place called heaven. You remember, when she said it, after your mum's funeral on the bench in the garden of remembrance?

I turned to the wall and put my fingers in my ears.

(A shout): Adam.

What, what do you want? You're scaring me. (I'd wet myself.)

(Calm again): There is no heaven. There's no such thing as heaven. I'm not living on anywhere. I'm dead in the ground; and there are ants and maggots and worms and they're eating me, eating my flesh, right now as we speak, and they are crawling all over me and eating what's left of me.

If that's true, why are you standing in front of me now? Why are you torturing me like this?

(A wicked laugh): I am a figment of your imagination. A figment of your fucked-up head. I'm not real.

Go away and leave me alone.

They came in again. They saw the wet bed; and they took me, stripped me, and put me in the shower. I sat on the floor, the water falling over my body, and I cried. They had to wash me. I don't even know who it was, maybe Damian. They washed me, then they took me back, dried me, and put me in fresh clothes.

In my clean bed, they left me, walking away, leaving me alone again and he was still there, still in the corner, still staring at me. Crawling up his legs were worms, and the maggots, and the ants. They crawled up his torso, across his shoulders, over his face and they covered him. They engulfed him while he laughed, and laughed, and laughed, and then he choked. He choked and he fell to the floor, and he couldn't move because they were all over him.

'Stop it, stop it, stop it, stop it.'

They gave me another injection and I fell asleep.

I woke up screaming.

The room was quiet and dense. My breathing was heavy. I paced. My body wouldn't allow me to sit. The pain was weighing me down, making me light, making me dizzy, making me sick. I was sick, lots and lots, until there was nothing left to come out of me.

I was banging my head against the wall when they brought my dad in. My fists clenched.

'Adam,' he cried. His hand to his mouth, he fell to his knees and he cried out. 'Do something for him, please, do something for him.'

They said: Anti-psychotics. Benzodiazepines. Constant monitoring.

'What's happening to him?' He was crying. 'What's happening to my son?'

They said: A psychotic episode. Psychological trauma. Post-traumatic stress syndrome.

He touched my shoulder. I turned and screamed in his face. Told him to fuck off.

They took him away.

'Take him away, take him away, he's useless anyway, he's useless.'

I went to sleep.

A massive crash woke me up. Like metal cutlery falling all over the floor. There was a knife on the floor of my room.

I picked it up.

(Jake's voice): What you doing with that, Adam?

The knife was in my hand, my hand was shaking.

Jab. Jab. Jab.

No, not three jabs, it was just one jab. Nathan did it with just one jab.

'Nathan. Why did you do it? We were so happy.'

(From the corner): This is a police announcement, put the knife on the floor and put your hands in the air. NOW.

I dropped the knife. It made a screaming noise.

(Behind me): I'm arresting you on suspicion of leaving your best friend to die. You do not have to say anything but anything you do say—

'Shut up, shut up, shut up.'

What sort of person leaves his best friend there to die? What sort of person would do that?

'A coward. A coward. A coward. I'm a coward. I'm weak. I'm weak. I'm weak.'

(A doctor): Give him something stronger. I need a syringe.

'Give me something stronger, give him the syringe. Give him the syringe.'

A scream.

Not mine.

(Debbie): Why did you leave him there, Adam, my baby, my baby, my baby?

A sharp scratch then everything went black.

I woke soaked in my own sweat. I was shivering. There were

arms around me. Someone was lying next to me on the bed. Holding me close.

A smell I knew.

Coconut shampoo.

I looked down to my chest. I knew those hands, that ring.

Let it be real. Let her be real.

(Her voice): It's OK, baby, it's OK. Everything is going to be OK.

Debbie. She's come. She's come to forgive me.

Her hand stroked my hair. She held me tight.

Please let her be real.

'Adam, your dad is here.' It was Damian.

She was gone.

He was there.

My eyes wouldn't focus. They were rolling into the back of my head.

'Where's she gone?'

'Who?'

'Debbie.'

'Debbie isn't here, son, it's me. It's your dad.'

'No! No!'

'Can't you give him something else?'

'He's had a maximum dose,'

'I want Debbie.'

'This isn't right, you must be able to do something else for him.'

'I want Debbie.'

'Adam, Debbie can't come.'

'I want Debbie.'

'Just lie down and go to sleep, you need to sleep.'

I did as they said. I slept. I slept, and I slept, and I slept.

When I finally opened my eyes, there were people in my room. A few, I think. Dad was there; David, too?

Someone else. Someone else was there with them.

I couldn't see who, my eyes wouldn't focus.

'Do something, do something. Do something for him. Oh Adam. Oh Adam.'

169

It was her. Her voice. She was back.

Debbie.

She was there, she was crying, she was reaching out to me, but I knew she wasn't real.

My mind was tricking me again, getting my hopes up, playing games.

I knew she wasn't real. She hated me. She would never forgive me for leaving Jake there.

'Oh Chris, I'm so sorry.' She was crying on my dad's shoulder. He was green like he was sick, like he hadn't slept for weeks, and weeks, and weeks.

'Go away. Stop playing tricks on me.'

'Oh Adam, my poor baby, Adam.'

I moved off the bed. I sat in the corner facing the wall. I had to ignore her. She wasn't real, I was just crazy.

I just had to ignore her.

She was touching my shoulder.

'Go away, you're not real.'

'Adam, I need you to turn around and look at me.'

She was touching my shoulder but she wasn't real.

'Adam, turn around slowly.'

'He's been having hallucinations, he thinks you're not real.'

Shut up, Dad.

'Adam, it's me, it's Debbie. Turn around, sweetheart, let me see you.'

'You're not real. You're in my head.'

'I am real, darling. Turn around and see me, turn around now.'

She was stroking my hair, like she did the time I was sick in the night when Jake and I were having a sleepover. I'd thrown up all over Jake's floor.

'Come on, baby, turn around now. I won't hurt you, you know I won't hurt you.'

'You hate me, you've just come to tell me how much you hate me.'

'Now now, don't be silly. I've come to see how you are, that's all.'

'I don't believe you.'

170

She moved me slowly round to face her and she was there, right in front of me. I could feel her breath on my face.

She took my hand and put it on her cheek. 'It's me, I'm here, I'm real.'

I stared at her. She was breathing. She was blinking and there were tears pouring out of her eyes, over her cheeks, and collecting in the corner of her mouth.

She'd come.

A wail came from deep inside me as her arms wrapped around me and I collapsed into her, sobbing.

Thirteen

David closed my notepad and put it on his lap. He rested his hands on it like he was protecting it, or what was inside it.

I sat up in bed, eating the toast Damian had brought me, and I watched David's face for signs of a reaction to all the stuff I'd told him. His face was straight. There was no emotion to be read. I guessed he was trained to be neutral, but I still needed to know what he thought, if he judged me, if he was about to walk away from me, no longer wanting to help me get better.

I wanted to ask him, but the words still wouldn't come out. I also wanted to ask him if Debbie had really been there. I remembered falling asleep in her arms, I don't know, maybe a few days ago. I'd lost track. All I knew was that when I'd woken up, all the crazy stuff had gone. The numbness was sort of back, but it felt different. I felt a bit clearer, a bit lighter. That horrible feeling that I was going to explode at any point had gone and I was so glad.

'Do you want some more?' David asked as I finished the last bite of my toast.

I shook my head.

He nodded. Then he pulled his chair a little bit closer. 'You know that you were talking during your episode, don't you?'

I shrugged. I wasn't too surprised to hear him say that because things were pretty mental for a while.

David looked defeated. I was certain he was going to get up and walk away and I wouldn't have blamed him. I was a lost cause. I could have told him that right from the very start. If I could have spoken I would have told him not to bother, that it was hopeless.

'I'm going to get Damian to come in and help you shower,' he said. 'I'll see you a bit later on.'

At that point, I knew he'd given up on me. Maybe because he realised it was hopeless. Or maybe he hated me too, for running off and leaving my best friend to die.

When I was fresh out the shower, Damian took me straight to the visitors' room and sat me down with a pot of tea and two mugs.

Two mugs.

As soon as I sat on one of the leather sofas, the door opened. David was there. He held it open for her as she walked in.

She moved slowly across the room. I wanted to get up and fling myself into her arms but I didn't, I sat, and watched her. She moved differently from how I remembered. The spring in her step had gone. Her eyes didn't shine the way they used to.

She looked broken and worn out.

David gestured for her to take a seat on the sofa. She sat down slowly and David sat next to her. I could see she was shaking, and I was, too. I found it hard that someone I'd always been so comfortable around could make me so scared and so nervous but I didn't blame her, it was my fault. I'd left her son, my best friend, on his own to die. If I'd stayed with him and saved his life, we wouldn't have been here right now. We would have been at home, like normal, comfortable in each other's company, and laughing and joking like we always had.

She couldn't look at me as she helped herself to a cup of tea. Tea wasn't her thing, it was coffee, and I wanted to ask Damian to get her one, but I couldn't move or speak or tear my eyes away from her.

Her reaction to me now made me believe even more that she hadn't come the other day, and that her holding me tight and me falling asleep while she stroked my hair was just in my head. A fantasy. Wishful thinking.

She gave a big sigh, then she looked up at me, and I braced myself for what she was about to say. I didn't think it was going to be good.

She tucked her hair behind her ear. 'You're not talking

again?' she asked. Her voice shook. 'You were talking the other day. You've stopped?'

So she had been there. I hadn't been imagining it.

'Adam, how did it get like this?'

I put my head down.

'I'd give anything to have you three boys back at my kitchen table, fighting over the best piece of chicken, or arguing over which flavour of Angel Delight we were having for pudding,' she said. She turned to David. 'Did you know I used to have to make three different flavours, just to keep the peace?'

David smiled but said nothing.

'I keep asking myself why it happened, Adam, how it happened. I can't understand it, none of it makes sense.' She picked up her cup, took a small sip and put it back on the table. She pushed mine closer towards me. 'Drink it or it'll get cold,' she said but there was a flat tone to her voice: not the usual pushy, but loving. Not the whole fed up but full of affection thing she always used to do.

I did as I was told.

'You know, Adam, I still go to talk to him, then I remember that he's gone, and ...' she paused. 'And I still go to talk to you, too. Some days, I make to go into the front room to check you're both OK, or if you want anything, but you're not there. The curtains are open, and it doesn't smell like boys, and the TV isn't blaring out some sort of crappy reality show or cartoons, and I wish so hard that it was.' She stopped to catch her breath.

I could feel the emotion circling in my stomach and I knew that I had to hold it in. I had no right to cry in front of her after what I'd done.

'I read up on it on the internet, you know,' she said. She reached into her bag for a tissue, and dabbed her eyes even though there were no tears. 'I read that if his artery was severed, he would have lost so much blood, that it wouldn't have taken long for him to die.'

'Do you mind me speaking?' David asked Debbie.

'No, of course,' she said.

'Adam is under the impression that if he hadn't left Jake, he
175

would have been able to save his life, but if what you're saying is true, then …'

I felt like I'd been punched in the stomach, I stood up and tried to catch my breath but I couldn't. I tried to stop the emotion, I tried to fight it, but I couldn't. I let go. I let go of everything that was inside me, and I hunched over, and this cry or scream or something just came flying out of me.

Debbie's hand went over her mouth, then she leant forward, reaching out to me. 'Adam,' she cried. 'No, Adam, you wouldn't have been able to save him.'

I was clutching my chest. I didn't know what it was that I was feeling. I couldn't compose myself, though, no matter how hard I tried.

David led me back to sit down. Debbie got up and sat next to me. She put her arms around me and I buried my face into the crook of her neck, and let my shaking body sink into the sofa.

I wouldn't have been able to save him. Even if I hadn't run off. 'I wouldn't have been able to save him. I wouldn't have been able to save him.'

'Adam?' Debbie pulled me away from her and looked at me. 'What did you say? Tell me again.'

'I wouldn't have been able to save him,' I said, then I pushed her off me and I was up and out of the chair and pacing like there was so much energy inside my body.

'I thought, I thought that because they said they'd tried to save him that he was still alive when he got to the hospital; and that if I'd stayed and stemmed the bleeding or something then …' I was talking so fast and I couldn't stop. 'Then I could have saved him and he'd still be here–'

'Deep breaths, Adam,' David said. 'Damian, can you get him some water, please?'

Debbie got up and took my hand tightly in hers. 'Amy, the girl who found him, she was at the hospital with us, do you remember?' She asked.

I nodded.

'She said afterwards that she couldn't find a pulse, and that they tried to restart his heart in the ambulance. She didn't want to say at the time because she didn't want us to worry. I don't know what happened when he got to the hospital, if they carried on trying or what, all I know is that if his artery was cut, it wouldn't have taken him long to die,' she said.

I thought back to the fight and tried to work out how long it was between Nathan stabbing Jake, and me running and it would have been a minute, two at the most. Jake had already stumbled to the bench and couldn't talk.

'He must have lost consciousness as soon as I'd run off,' I said. I wiped my eyes with my hands and let the thought sit in my head. 'But I shouldn't have left him,' I said. 'I still shouldn't have left him.'

Debbie let go of my hand. She reached into her handbag and handed me some tissues. 'I'm not sure I should say this, but I'm going to anyway,' she said. She took a deep breath. 'Every day I wish you hadn't. Every day I wish he hadn't died on his own, that you were there holding his hand and pretending to him that everything was going to be OK.' She stopped to compose herself. 'He was my baby, and he shouldn't have died alone on that cold, wet bench, Adam, he shouldn't have died alone.' She couldn't hold her sobs in anymore and neither could I.

'I'd go back if I could,' I said desperately. 'I'd go back, and I'd stay with him, and I'd talk to him about anything I could to distract him,' I said. I walked away from the sofa. It was too much to take in.

'You OK?' David asked. Damian handed me a cup of water but I pushed it away.

I shook my head. I tried to push the image of Jake collapsed on the bench, our bench, the place we'd shared so many happy times. I wished so hard I could go back there, to that day. If there was nothing I could have done to stop it happening, at least I would have been with him when he took his last breath.

'Why did I have to be so weak?' I said. 'Why did I have to run off with Nathan? Why couldn't I have stayed? Why?' I cried, but I knew that nobody had the answer to that question, not even me.

'You know what I ask myself?' Debbie looked up at me. 'I ask myself why I didn't stop you two going to that bloody party. I knew how anxious you were about it. I knew that as we ate dinner because you were both so quiet. Every day I sit and ask myself why I didn't stop you. Why I didn't suggest that we rent a movie, and why I didn't lure you into staying with all your favourite sweets and massive hot chocolates with whipped cream and marshmallows.'

'But it's not your fault,' I said.

'I was his mother, Adam,' she said with so much force. 'I was meant to protect him. I should have done more. I should have listened to you when you sat and told me how worried you were about Nathan changing. I should have known there was something wrong and I should have helped you both, talked to you so you knew how to handle it, but I didn't. I brushed it off. I didn't think anything like this would happen.'

'Neither did I,' I said.

'And that's the problem, isn't it?' She said. 'We never think something like this will happen to *us*, not to us.'

Debbie sat back down, defeated, and David guided me to sit next to her. She took my hand.

'It's all well and good us both sitting here, saying that we would have done this or that to stop it and we can blame ourselves for it all day long, but it's not going to change anything, is it?'

I shook my head.

'Do you think Jake would blame you, really? Because if you do, you don't know him as well as you think you did,' she said. 'He worshipped the ground you walked on, Adam.'

I screwed up my face to try and stop the tears escaping, but I couldn't stop them.

'You have a choice, Adam,' she said. 'You can sink or you can swim. You can get up, every morning, even though you don't want to, and you can carry on. You can do it for Jake, because that's what he would have wanted, or you can give up. You can go home and take all those tablets and you can give up on life.' She was cross with me now.

I sat back, put my hands over my face, and cried.

'You want to get out of here and take all those tablets? Well, that's your choice, but I think it's selfish. Jake's life was taken away from him. He didn't have a choice in the matter.'

She pulled my hands away and turned my head to face her, so I couldn't avoid her eyes. 'You do have a choice Adam, so what are you going to do? What are you going to decide?'

I collapsed into her shoulder and cried more. She pulled me closer and held me tight. 'There's no way he'd have wanted you to give up, Adam,' she whispered in my ear.

I knew she was right and even though the pain flooding out of me was overwhelming, I knew I had to find some fight from somewhere. I had to carry on.

Fourteen

I was lost without my pad and with nothing else to write. I asked the nurse what she was doing. She smiled and handed me her puzzle book and pen. When I saw it was Sudoku, I handed it back.

'I'm bored, not desperate,' I said, and she laughed.

'You know how good it is to hear that beautiful voice of yours.'

Right on cue, Josie appeared in the doorway with a huge smile on her face. She was hopping from one foot to the other. She looked like she was going to explode with excitement.

'Damian said we can go outside for a bit, he's going to take us for some fresh air,' she said. 'Get your shoes on.'

'OK,' I said, and she squealed.

The afternoon was warm and sunny.

'Spring has sprung, my chickens,' Damian said, holding his face up to the air and breathing in deeply through his nose. 'Smell that?' He asked.

'Yeah, it's pollen.' Josie winked at me.

'Such a pessimist,' Damian groaned at her. 'What am I going to do with you?' He asked.

'I've got hayfever,' she said. 'You can't hold that against me.'

'Fair enough,' he said, and got his newspaper out.

We sat down on a bench opposite his and Josie got her tobacco out. I watched her roll a cigarette and waited for her to roll me one, but she didn't.

'He knows you don't smoke,' she said.

Damian rolled his eyes.

'What was it like when you went all wacko?' She asked. 'You were screaming your lungs out; we heard it in the rec room. I was really worried.'

'It was strange, I felt like I was on a different planet. Like I was there but I wasn't, it's hard to explain.'

'How are you feeling now, though?'

'Better, I think. I mean I got it all out, the stuff I was burying down and trying to hide from.'

'David's good,' she said.

'David's a genius,' Damian added.

'I still feel guilty, though,' I said.

'You will, but I don't think you should,' Josie said. 'I mean, had anyone ever sat you down and told you what to do if something like that happened?' She asked. 'It's not like you ever had a lesson of "what to do if a fight breaks out and your mate gets stabbed" in between maths and double PE.'

'True.'

'Exactly,' she said. 'Then how the hell were you meant to know what to do? You did what was natural. It's like fight or flight, isn't it? Your fear took over and you ran. I bet you any money anyone else would have done the same thing.'

'I wish I hadn't,' I said.

'That's what you're going to have to work on with David,' Damian piped up. 'He'll help you. He's not going to let you out of his sight until he knows you're going to be OK.'

'And I'm here, too,' Josie said. 'I don't know if that helps or anything, but I am.'

I couldn't help but question her motives still. I didn't understand why she cared so much about me when she hardly knew me. Josie was waiting for a reaction. I had to be careful how I worded it. I didn't want to upset her.

Why do you care so much?' I asked her.

She took a pull on her cigarette and blew out some smoke rings. 'Honestly, I don't know – I just do.' she said.

'It's a bit strange.'

'You know what I think? I think that sometimes you just care. Sometimes you don't need a reason.'

'Quite philosophical, Jose. I might have to write that one

down,' Damian said.

'You do that,' she winked at him.

I didn't know what to say. I thought back to the day Jake and I made friends with Nathan. He could have been thinking the same thing as I was now. He could have been wondering why Jake and I cared. Maybe that was how it worked; maybe some people just become friends by accident. Maybe it just happens.

'I'm sorry for grassing you up that day,' she said. 'I just didn't want you to …'

'I know,' I said. I'd never met anyone like her before. She was so troubled, so broken, but at the same time she had the biggest heart.

'Right, come on you two, we better get back in before they send out a search party. Plus, I'm going to nip out and get some cake and stuff for you all.'

We stood up to go back inside. Josie linked her arm in mine. 'Fancy a game of pool?' She asked. 'I can teach you how to play properly.'

'Go on, then,' I said. And this time, I actually wanted to.

Josie was just about to beat me for the third time in a row when I felt like we were being watched. When I turned around, David was standing at the nurses' station with his arms folded and a small smile on his face. If I didn't know any better, I'd say he looked a bit smug.

When he saw me looking, he pointed and beckoned.

He took me into the staff kitchen where there were some supermarket carrier bags full of cakes and treats.

'Thought I'd give you first pick before the vultures get to them,' he smiled. 'You've not yet had the pleasure of experiencing cake day. It's like the gold rush all over again.'

I rifled through the bags while he put the kettle on. I picked out a tub of chocolate brownies and David said we could share them as they were his favourites, too.

We walked down to the therapy room and made ourselves comfortable with the tea and brownies.

'So how are you feeling?' He asked.

'Strange,' I said.

'Can you elaborate?'

'I feel lighter, but I still feel like there's a dark cloud over my head.'

'What do you think has made you feel lighter?' He leant back and crossed his legs.

'Definitely knowing that it wasn't my fault he died,' I said.

'And how do you feel about what Debbie said, about fighting? Have you made a decision?'

I took a deep breath. 'I'm going to fight,' I said. 'For Jake and for myself.'

'I can imagine it makes you feel secure knowing that she's here for you?'

'Definitely.'

David's face turned serious. 'Do you have any idea why Nathan used the knife? When you caught up with him, did he tell you?'

'No,' I said. 'He was panicked, and Sarah was in a massive state. He told me to take her home, go home myself, and not say anything to anyone. That was the last time I saw him.'

'Why do you think he did it?'

'I don't know. I've thought about it so much but I can't work it out. Danny didn't put him up to it … Even he didn't know. He was so shocked when he saw Jake had been stabbed, I'll never forget the look on his face.'

'Do you know what happened after you left the party? What made Nathan think Jake took his phone?'

'Apparently, Danny wanted to get off his decks and asked Nathan to get his phone to put in the dock. Nathan couldn't find it anywhere. Lucy turned up and told them she thought she saw Jake with it. I didn't even know we'd passed her on our way out or to the park.'

'And Jake didn't have Nathan's phone?'

'Of course not. Danny found it down the back of the sofa when he was cleaning up from the party.'

'So why do you think Lucy said that?'

'Because of what happened that day in the park, I guess. She'd warned Jake that he'd regret being rude to her. I don't know if she realised it'd get out of hand like that, maybe she just wanted to cause a bit of a row?'

'How many of them were arrested for Joint Enterprise that night?'

'I don't know exactly, but Danny, Sarah, and Lucy I know for sure.'

'Think about what Joint Enterprise means, Adam. You can be responsible for someone's death just by being there and encouraging it, even if you didn't do the stabbing yourself.'

I didn't know where he was going with it.

'You weren't arrested, were you? You were only taken in for questioning and let straight back out with no charge, right?'

I nodded.

'So can you see, now, that a lot of people had a part to play in what happened that night, and are actually responsible, but none of those people were you.'

I guessed he was right. The chain of events in the run-up to what happened involved a lot of people.

'Who's really to blame for Jake's death, Adam?'

'Nathan,' I said.

'He was the one who made the decision to stab him in the leg. He'll have to live with it for the rest of his life,' David said in a very matter-of-fact tone.

'You did nothing, as far as I can see, to contribute to it happening. Does that make you feel any better?'

'Yeah, but,' I stopped. 'I still should have been with him,' I said.

David nodded. He leant over and opened the tub of brownies, took one, then gestured for me to.

'Do you want to know what my plan is?' He asked.

I nodded.

'Do you know what post-traumatic stress syndrome is?'

'Isn't that the thing the soldiers get when they come back from war?' I wondered what that had to do with me.

'Yes, but there are other things that can trigger it, too, such as what has happened to you. Your symptoms, like the nightmares, the panic attacks, the fact that by the time you got here, you'd completely shut down, it's a definite diagnosis,' he said.

'So what do we do?' I asked.

'We're going to do something called Eye Movement Desensitisation and Reprocessing,' he said. 'What and the what what what?' I asked. It had gone straight over the top of my head.

He laughed. 'Basically, I get you to recall the event and, while you're doing that, I get you to do a series of eye movements. It helps to reprogramme your brain so that the distressing memories have less of an influence over your head,' he said. He offered me another brownie.

'That sounds complicated,' I said.

He smiled. 'I am also drafting in a colleague of mine called Sandra. She's a grief counsellor and she is wonderful, you're going to love her,' he said. 'Her job is going to be to help you find ways to manage your grief for Jake,' he paused.

'I don't know if I will, it seems impossible and really overwhelming.'

'All in good time,' he said. 'You're not out of the woods yet, but we'll get you there.'

'Do you know how long I'm going to be in here for?' I asked.

'As long as it takes,' he said. 'But now you're communicating and more stable, you can get involved in the life on the ward and you can voice your needs, so if things do get too much, you can tell us straight away.'

'OK, but I don't want to do music therapy – it's awful,' I said.

He laughed. 'Yes, I heard about the incident with Caitlin, Blake, and the drumstick.'

'I need you to know, Adam, that you're going to have your good days and your bad days and I don't want you to put too much pressure on yourself to get better. It's OK if you're not. Just make sure you tell one of us?'

'I will.'

'Good. I'm going to keep you on the medication you're on for now, too, but I will wean you off it as and when I feel the time is right.' He picked up his mug and took a sip of his tea. 'I've decided to keep your dad at a distance for now, too,' he said.

'Thank you.'

'Anymore questions?'

'Yeah, has Polly been in?' I asked.

'I was wondering when you were going to ask me that.' He smiled.

Fifteen

Polly stood at the nurses' station with a rucksack over her shoulder, a giant bin bag at her feet, and a supermarket carrier bag in her hand. I wondered if she was moving in.

I bounced over to her from where I'd been sitting with some of the others, watching an old Western movie on the TV in the rec room. I was smiling but she wasn't. I immediately stopped bouncing and walked slowly and cautiously.

We stood and eyed each other up for a second.

'You stopped being bat shit crazy yet?' She asked.

I laughed. 'Nah, I thought I'd carry it on for a while,' I said.

Her face cracked into a huge smile. 'I've brought you some stuff,' she said. 'Shall we go to your room?'

'Hold your horses,' Damian said, skidding over from where he was plonked on the floor with the rest of them watching the film. 'I have to come with you and check it all first.'

'Why?' Polly asked in her normal 'defensive towards the whole world' tone. 'I thought he was off suicide watch?'

'He is, but I still need to withhold any sharp objects, and I also need to go through that.' He pointed at the supermarket carrier bag.

'You want to see if there's any good food in there you can steal, don't you?' Josie said, appearing at my side.

'Busted.' He laughed.

Josie took a step towards Polly and introduced herself. Polly looked her up and down, and for a moment I braced myself.

'Nice to meet you,' she said and smiled.

'Come on then, you two,' Damian said.

As we went to walk off, Josie grabbed my arm. 'Is that your

girlfriend?' She asked. 'She's really pre–'

'I saw her first,' I said, cutting in.

'Just saying,' she smiled and went back over to the rec room.

Polly emptied the bin bag first. There were two cushions and a blanket. To make things a bit more homely, she told me. 'Unless you think he's going to try and smother himself with them?' She asked Damian. I cringed.

'It's a well-known fact you can't smother yourself,' he said. 'But nice sarcasm,' he winked.

She rolled her eyes. 'Debbie sent that in,' she said, as Damian opened the rucksack.

'Is she not coming back in?' I asked, panicked.

'Yeah, she is, it's just she can't make it today and I said I was, so she said to bring it so you had some clean stuff,' she said.

'Why can't she come in today?' I asked.

'She's gone to get a puppy,' she said.

'A puppy?'

'Yep, she said she needed something to do, someone to look after. She showed me a picture of her, she's gorgeous.'

'Which breed?' Damian asked.

'Labrador,' Polly said bluntly. She was yet to warm to Damian.

When Damian had emptied out the rucksack full of brand-new clothes Debbie had bought, and some toiletries and stuff, he gave us the OK and left us alone to talk.

'I'm just going to come out with this and say it,' Polly said with her hands on her hips. 'Do you still want to kill yourself?' She asked.

I sat down on my bed and looked at the floor.

'That's a yes, then?'

'No, it's not,' I said. 'Do you have to be like this?' I looked up at her.

'Like what?'

'This,' I said.

'Oh, so you've got your voice back,' she said. 'But you're using it to be rude.'

'You're the one being rude,' I said.

'Yeah, well,' she said, but she wasn't looking at me. 'You went bloody mental, Adam. God, I want to knock you out right now.'

'Why?' I asked.

She was looking at her feet. 'Because I've been so worried about you.'

I didn't know what to say. When I saw her last she was timid, frail, and full of tears. Now she was being stroppy. I wondered if it was just a defensive thing.

She sighed and sat on the edge of my bed. The silence was thick. I wanted to reach out to her but I didn't know how.

'Do you want me around?' She asked.

'Yes,' I said.

'Good,' she said.

We still didn't move. We were sitting next to each other with a space between us. It was only a small space, but it felt like a huge gap. I wanted to shuffle towards her to feel closer to her, but it wasn't happening.

'Ed sent this lot in,' she said, picking up the carrier bag and opening it.

It was full of crisps and chocolate bars and stuff.

'He said he can come and see you if you want.'

'Cool,' I said.

'What's the deal with that Josie then?' She asked.

I plumped up the new cushions she'd brought me and put them up by my pillow, then I wiggled up and lay back against them. They felt good. Soft. Comfy. Polly took the blanket and covered her lap with it. She grabbed two packets of crisps out the bag, threw one at me and opened the other for herself.

'She's OK,' I said. 'I'm not really sure.'

'What's wrong with her?'

'She self-harms and says her parents put her in here because she's a lesbian,' I said.

Polly looked like all the muscles in her body suddenly relaxed.

I laughed.

'What?'

'Were you jealous?'

191

She snorted.

'You were jealous,' I said.

She looked me square in the eye and smiled. 'I'm not expecting anything from you, Ads,' she said. 'That was the one thing Ed said to me, that I couldn't expect anything from you 'cause if I did, it might put too much pressure on you.'

'I do want you to visit, though,' I said.

'I'm going to anyway,' she poked her tongue out at me. 'There's something else I brought you,' she said. 'I wasn't sure if I should or not, but I think it'll be OK.'

'What?'

She opened her bag and pulled out a picture frame. It was the one of my mum from my bedside table. 'Is it OK?' she asked.

I sighed to try and stop the tears welling up in my eyes.

'Adam?'

I looked at my mum's face. It seemed like a lifetime ago. So much had happened in such a short space of time. 'Thanks,' I whispered to Polly. I put the picture on the small shelf above my bed.

'I thought it might remind you that she'll still be around, like an angel,' she said. She touched my hand gently.

'I hope so,' I said. 'I miss her.'

'There's something else,' Polly said. She went to reach into her bag, but hesitated. I knew why. I knew what was coming next.

'Go on,' I said. 'It's OK.'

She pulled out the other picture. 'Keep him close,' she whispered as she held it out to me.

My hands were shaking as I took it from her. My heart ached from the inside out as I looked at the two of us, Jake and I, and our snowman Bobski.

'Wherever he is, do you think he hates me?' I asked.

'He'll always love you,' Polly said.

The tears came falling from my eyes.

'And he's probably taking the piss out of you for being such a pussy.' She laughed through her own tears.

'I wish he knew how sorry I was,' I said.

192

'Tell him,' she said. 'You never know, he might still be around.'

'Do you think?'

'Oh, come on,' she said, wiping her eyes with the sleeve of her jumper. 'He's probably waiting and biding his time for the perfect chance to haunt us all.'

I looked at the picture, at his face, and in my mind, I went straight back to that day; to screaming laughs, numb fingers, and pelting each other with snowballs. We were so young, so innocent. So happy.

I never thought in a million years that it would come to an end.

'You OK?' Polly asked.

I held the picture to my chest. 'I miss him so much, Pol,' I said.

'I bet he misses you more,' she said. She moved her body next to mine and she took my head and held it to her chest. My body shook with the tears and I realised that the sadness was crushing. My heart was well and truly broken, into a million pieces.

'It's going to be OK,' she said into my hair. 'I'm not going to let you go.'

I caved into all my urges; I let all the fear of letting her be there for me go. I curled up into her and I cried for Jake, for my broken heart, and for all the future memories that we'd never get to make.

'I hate him,' I said.

'Who?'

'Who do you think?'

'I know,' she said softly. 'He's going to get his dues, though, he won't be getting out of that prison for a very long time.'

'It's not enough,' I said. 'It'll never be enough.'

I curled back in to her and my mind wandered to him. I wondered if he realised all the carnage he'd caused, all the hearts he'd broken, all the lives he'd ruined – and for what? I still didn't know why he did it. I don't think I'll ever know.

Jake was gone, but it wasn't just his life Nathan took away that night: each and every one of us connected to him had to live with what Nathan had done for the rest of our lives.

I wondered what he was doing now, if he knew, and if he was sorry.

Dear Jake,

I went to our bench today for the first time since that night. They've put a plaque on it: "In Loving Memory of Jake Coldridge", and it's got the day you were born and the day you died on it. When I saw it, my legs gave way underneath me, and Polly and Ed had to hold me up. They said it's a place I can always go to feel close to you, but I'm not sure if I will. It feels wrong sitting there now, without you. Especially knowing it was the place you took your last breath and knowing that I should have been there with you, holding your hand.

I've been out of the hospital for a week now, and I'm learning to take things one day at a time. There are good days and bad days, but there isn't a day where you're not the first thing I think about when I wake up in the morning.

I'm back home with Dad. Don't worry, I think he might have had a secret lobotomy while I was away. He's kicked Jackie to the kerb, he's stopped drinking, and he's even cleaned the house. He's not said sorry to me yet for any of it but I kind of figured out that, sometimes, actions are more important than words. I'd rather this than him saying sorry a thousand times over but not changing anything. The day I got back, he took me upstairs saying he had a surprise for me. He'd done up my bedroom: painted it, got all new furniture and curtains and everything. He'd actually listened to me when I said one day in a therapy session with him and David that I was frightened to go back to my old bedroom, because of all the bad memories. He even bought a new string for my guitar – well, he had to take Ed and Polly with him because he didn't know what to buy, but still. He said he nearly came out with a drum kit, as a hobby for himself, but he resisted. He said he'll try and get a job instead.

I went round to see your mum this morning. It was her who suggested I write a letter to you. When she asked me how I was feeling, now I was out, I said to her that there was so much I wanted to say to you but I'd never get the chance. She told me she'd been writing to you. She leaves the letters on your pillow, just in case you come back at all. She said you'd see them there.

That's where I'm going to leave this one.

When I was still in the hospital, I asked her what it felt like for her, because I wondered if she felt the same things I did. She told me it was like she was in a car, being driven by someone else through some really scary, high-up mountain roads. She said she's in the back with you and you're holding on to each other for dear life. When the car goes round a sharp bend, she closes her eyes because she's so scared. When she opens them, the car door is open and you're gone. You've fallen out the car and down the mountain and she's screaming at the driver to stop so she can go and get you, but he won't. You're gone and there's nothing she can do about it. Nothing at all.

She's strong, Jake, really strong – but she's broken. You can see it in her eyes. They don't have the same sparkle they used to. I worry about her, that she's on her own in the house and you're not there, but she says it's OK. She says it's too quiet without us running round, and getting on her nerves, so she keeps the radio or TV on all the time. She's got the puppy, Callie, to keep her occupied as well. She's six months old now and a proper terror. You'd be going mental if you could see her. She chews up everything and when you ring the doorbell, she goes crazy. Your mum said I can take Callie out for a walk at any time.

Polly, Ed, and I are going to go up to some little village in the Peak District soon, to see Josie. She got out a month before me. Her aunt, her mum's sister, said she could go and live with her and it's been amazing for her. She gets to be who she wants to be and she says she's got all that nature around her. Her aunt said we can go up and stay for the weekend, and Ed passed his driving test a couple of months ago, so we're going to have a road trip up there. I'm quite looking forward to it. Ed fancies the pants off her and flirted with her loads when he came in to see me. We decided not to tell him straight away that she's a total cock phobic (her words) to wind him up. When we eventually broke the news to him, Josie said she fancies Polly and they pretended to have a bit of a snog and Ed screeched and ran off, but I was quite turned on by it, if I'm honest. I don't reckon I'll let them do it again, though. I don't want to share my girlfriend with anyone.

Nathan's trial starts in the autumn. He's probably going to get manslaughter. I have to be a witness but I get to do it by video link and I am so glad, because I don't want to see him. I don't think I could see him and not hurt him the way he hurt you. I'm not going to say any more about him because I don't want to upset you.

I hope you don't hate me for leaving you there, Jake. I still wonder what you thought when I ran off. I'm hoping that what your mum said was right, and that the artery being cut would have meant you died quickly. You wouldn't have known you were dying, then. It would have been instant. You wouldn't have had time to get scared. Those are my only saving graces.

I need you to know now, though, how sorry I am. I should have been there, holding your hand as you left this world. I should have been telling you everything was going to be OK, or made some stupid joke or something, anything as long as I was there. I'll never forgive myself for it. Every time I think about it, even now, my stomach fills with dread but I've come to terms with the fact I'll never get over that, I just have to learn to live with it.

I honestly never thought I would lose you, Jake. I think we all seem to have it in our heads that we're immortal when we're not. Anything can happen, at any time, and I really don't think I ever told you how much you meant to me. I didn't need to, did I? In my head, you were never going anywhere.

I'll tell you now. You meant the world to me, Jake. We never went a day without seeing each other and you were always, always there for me when I needed you. You stuck up for me without question, even if you thought I was wrong. You looked after me. You made me laugh all the time, even when you weren't trying. You even shared your mum with me. There's this huge Jake-shaped hole in my life now, but I will always hold you in my heart. I fucking loved you, man, more than you'll ever know. I can't believe you're gone, Jake. It still doesn't seem real. I still keep expecting you to pop out at any moment, and tell me you were only joking and congratulate yourself for pulling the biggest prank of your life on me. I'd give anything to have just one more hour with you. Just so I could see you one more time.

I know I can't, so I have to go now. I've got a whole world waiting for me out there, and I know that you'd want me to go and live my life, so that's what I'm going to do, even though I'm crying at the thought of saying goodbye.

If you haven't already, go and find my mum up there in heaven. She'll look after you, just like yours is looking after me down here. And can you tell her I love her? And give her a kiss from me.

I miss you so much, man, but I'll definitely see you soon, yeah? Make sure you're there waiting for me, or I'm gonna come and find you, and kick your arse.

In the meantime, no flirting with the angels. Leave them alone. They're pure and don't need corrupting by you.

Love you, man. With everything I have.

Be good.

Adam xxx

With Special Thanks to

The Accent YA Blog Squad

Alix Long

Anisah Hussein

Anna Ingall

Annie Starkey

Becky Freese

Becky Morris

Bella Pearce

Beth O'Brien

Caroline Morrison

Charlotte Jones

Charnell Vevers

Claire Gorman

Daniel Wadey

Darren Owens

Emma Hoult

Fi Clark

Heather Lawson

James Briggs

With Special Thanks to

The Accent YA Blog Squad

James Williams

Joshua A.P

Karen Bultiauw

Katie Lumsden

Katie Treharne

Kieran Lowley

Laura Metcalfe

Lois Acari

Maisie Allen

Mariam Khan

Philippa Lloyd

Rachel Abbie

Rebecca Parkinson

Savannah Mullings-Johnson

Sofia Matias

Sophia

Toni Davis

With Special Thanks to

The Accent YA Editor Squad

Aishu Reddy

Alice Brancale

Amani Kabeer-Ali

Anisa Hussain

Barooj Maqsood

Ellie McVay

Grace Morcous

Katie Treharne

Miriam Roberts

Rebecca Freese

Sadie Howorth

Sanaa Morley

Sonali Shetty

For more information about **Natalie Flynn**

and other Young Adult titles from

Accent YA

please visit

www.accentya.com